Bearers of the Sun

Bearers of the Sun

Chris Foster

Integrity International
Publishing Company

P.O. Box 9, 100 Mile House
British Columbia, Canada V0K 2E0

2nd Printing, 1985

Canadian Cataloguing in Publication Data

Foster, Chris, 1932-
Bearers of the sun

ISBN 0-9690341-2-1

I. Title.
PS8561.087B42 1984 C813'.54 C84-091357-5
PR9199.3.F68B42 1984

Printed in Canada

To all who sense a larger destiny

Bearers of the Sun

Chapter I

Passage From the Sun

Pirius, bearer of the spirit of persistence, voiced the question.

They sat—four close friends—in the garden of the Central Palace, waiting to be called. No words could describe the richness of the colours that surrounded the Palace. When High Council is in session, those twelve beings who compose the focus of authority for the Sun and all its integrated systems, even the walls and grounds glow with extraordinary intensity.

"I wonder if we will find each other while we are on the earth?" Pirius asked.

"It is true that we may be continents apart," said Haldan. "But I trust the compulsions of Mazzaroth to bring us together."

"Yes indeed," said the beautiful Mirana, nodding her golden head. "It will happen. I feel it in the core of my being. What do you think, Magnabaran?" She turned to the remaining member of the group.

Magnabaran's noble features softened as he met her gaze.

"It is obviously vital that we do meet on this occasion," he said simply. His voice was quiet, but vibrant with authority.

"Events are coming to a head on earth very quickly. Without doubt we approach a time of climax."

"The time to which we have all looked with such longing," said Mirana softly, "when the unhappy state that human beings have created would pass away and order and beauty be established again on the planet we love."

It was not possible for Mirana to be serious too long. Her delight burst forth. "How wonderful that we shall be incarnate at the same time," she cried. "What an adventure it will be!"

As if touched by her enthusiasm a small cluster of shimmering creatures, jewels of violet and gold, flew close and began to sing. They were joined instantly by the chanting of many trees.

From where they sat near the entrance to the conference chamber, the four sun beings had a clear view of the graceful columns and domes of the distant Palace of Uranus, and the luminous arches of the Palace of Neptune. All around, trees and flowers shone brightly. There were no shadows, for in the City of the Sun all seeing is radiant seeing, and all objects are radiant objects.

A portal of the Central Palace opened and Jalina, assistant to senior Council member Lord Perakleos, came towards them. The aura of green and blue surrounding Jalina fairly crackled with excitement. Nonetheless her voice, as she spoke, was calm, filled with the sweet music that permeates the expression of all those who inhabit the Sun.

"Please. It is time for you to come." Jalina's eyes bespoke her love for the four beings whom she addressed. "Lord Mi-om-Ra and the Council wish to spend a few moments with you."

As they walked toward the Palace, Magnabaran was aware of his love and respect for Mi-om-Ra, and those who sat on the Council, kindling and rising like a flame within him. This was not the love of one being for another deemed to be greater or separate. It was a perception and affirmation of oneness, a oneness that reached beyond the borders of time, having its roots in eternity.

The four, accompanied by Jalina, passed through the Palace portal and walked along a corridor into a conference chamber. The atmosphere alternately brightened and softened as a variety of colours pulsed and ebbed within the room. Supreme Lord Mi-om-Ra waited until the four were seated. Gradually a white light of indescribable purity and incandescence enveloped the room, drawing all present together. Mi-om-Ra's voice seemed to be a living prism that filled the chamber with radiance.

"Welcome," he said, looking at Magnabaran, Pirius, Haldan and Mirana. It was just one word, but it conveyed tremendous warmth. "I am delighted that we have this opportunity to commune together in person before you go."

Mi-om-Ra paused, and there was silence, a silence alive with friendship and shared purpose. Presently he continued, his love palpable and all-enfolding.

"It is an unfortunate fact that with humankind in its present state, everyone grows up with the conviction of being merely human. Recently I commissioned Prince Tauhelion and his consort to incarnate on earth and remind earth's inhabitants of their true character and identity as incarnate sun beings. Unless a sufficient number do awaken to this, humankind cannot survive much longer. I would like the four of you to follow Tauhelion to earth as soon as possible and play a leadership part with him in this undertaking."

It was evident that Mi-om-Ra had completed his remarks. Queen Serenus, seated by his side, smiled at him and then at the four. "Our love will be with you," she said. Then, almost to herself, she added, "What does it take to wake humanity up?"

Everyone in the chamber knew what she meant, for they had seen the terrible ravages and suffering caused by what human beings were already calling their "First World War."

"They imagine themselves to be alone in a hostile universe," said Perakleos. "They are so taken up with their human designs and purposes that they have no awareness of our presence, even though without the sun being within they are nothing."

"Nothing but a corpse," interjected the outspoken Lord Diaxos.

There was a brief pause. Pirius spoke up. "Is it true that the earth will likely be at war again soon?" he asked.

Perakleos looked at Mi-om-Ra, to see if he wished to speak, then undertook to answer himself.

"It is very possible," he said. "Our conclusion is that the world will be torn by increasing conflict in the years ahead. This would include the likelihood of a second world war even more horrible and destructive than the first. Beyond that we sense a gigantic split coming between two phases of humanity, the East and West. This schism between male and female aspects will bind masses of people in fear and suspicion."

Mi-om-Ra spoke. "This is the state of confusion into which you and multitudes of our host must go," he said gravely. "It is sad to see humans bringing such suffering upon themselves, but if this is what it takes to cause them to wake up to the effects of their sorry behaviour then so must it be."

"Surely," said Haldan, "there will be many who will so awaken."

"I trust so," said Mi-om-Ra. "We cannot allow this wretched condition to continue indefinitely." A mischievous look suddenly came over his countenance. "I suppose," he said slowly, "we should consider some more down-to-earth matters? Please, Perakleos."

"The Council has been considering the thoughts that each of you have had about your coming incarnations," Perakleos said, taking his cue. "I believe, Magnabaran, that you had England in mind?"

"The upper class, no less," said Mirana, her eyes filled with fun. "Nothing but the best for Magnabaran."

"The champagne will not quite compare with this nectar from Queen Serenus' garden," said Magnabaran, looking at the goblet in front of him. "But it will be an improvement over my last venture to England many centuries ago when I had nothing to drink but dark and foul-tasting beer. Ugh!" His features took on a look of disgust. "But to be serious," he went on. "My feeling is that although the British Empire is likely to collapse before long, Britain will remain an important centre of stability with connections all around the planet which will be most useful to us."

Several members of the Council nodded their heads. "We agree," said Perakleos. He turned to Pirius. "This split between East and West that I mentioned has interesting implications," he went on. "We are especially concerned about the recent revolution in Russia. Our feeling is, dear Pirius, that we would rather have you there than in Australia. Your sensitive but persistent spirit will serve as a beacon for those who begin to awaken in that troubled land."

"I shall be delighted to go to Russia," said Pirius readily. "There is a great heart in that people crying out for true direction. It seems to me that despite his ideals, Lenin has opened the door to an awful tyranny which may prove worse than that of the Czars."

"Just what we were considering before you came in," said Perakleos.

It was the turn of Haldan and Mirana. "What are your thoughts for us?" they asked simultaneously.

Everyone on the High Council laughed heartily, and the chamber shimmered for a moment as if part of a mirage. "I can see you two will make a fine team," said Perakleos. "We like your thought about North America and would encourage you in that direction. There is an openness to new ideas and approaches in that land which is most useful from our standpoint. That is why we look for an initial thrust of awakening to occur on that continent, and why Tauhelion himself chose to incarnate there."

"He is doing well?" Magnabaran asked.

"Very well," replied Perakleos. "His physical form is presently at the boyhood stage, but showing a remarkable willingness to be honest and learn from mistakes. Tauhelion chose his parents wisely. They are not particularly important as human society judges in these things, but they are people of high vision and integrity who share an excellent relationship."

Lord Mi-om-Ra looked around him. His presence seemed to intensify and fill the chamber with blessing.

"This may be all we need to consider together at this time," he said. His gaze lingered on each of the four. "Go in strength upon your mission," he said softly. "We will be with you."

They passed upon their way like wind passing over a field of grain, leaving behind them only the impression of movement through colours known only in the sun. Gradually the music that imbues and interplays with those colours faded behind them. Like swimmers plunging into a deep mountain pool they descended into a place of darkness that is nonetheless a place of warmth and life: the womb of woman. There, each of them, Magnabaran, Haldan, Mirana and Pirius, blended the substance of the sun with the substance of the earth into a living whole to create four human forms. The waiting embryos now had life. As is the case with all human beings, the indwelling sun beings would provide all necessary purpose and direction. Absolutely trustworthy, they would never deny or betray the sacred responsibility which they had assumed. They would be present and watchful in every moment. Through the various stages of the evolution of their physical, human forms, they would offer such control, healing and protection as those forms would allow. Hopefully, from these tiny beginning points there might emerge mature persons in whom the blending of sun and earth would come to conscious fruition, and through whom the work of creative restoration might proceed . . .

By the human calendar it was during the months of July, August and September, in the year 1921, that Magnabaran and the others, four out of a vast number of their kind, took human form in the process known as incarnation.

Chapter II

1935

"Hey Pamela, look at this."

Judy Thorpe held out the prime piece of young birch bark that she had found. The silvery side of it gleamed in the bright summer sunshine.

The two of them had gone out collecting bark to make model canoes. Pamela Simpson looked over at Judy's find, but she had lost interest in what they were doing. She was busy watching a pair of loons playing hide and seek in the water. In her own imagination, at least, they were playing hide and seek. First one loon would poke up its bottom and dive beneath the surface, while the other paddled around looking for it; then they would change roles and the one that had done the hiding would become the seeker.

Pamela was vaguely aware of her friend dashing excitedly back into the woods to find some more bark. Then, as a canoe rounded the nearby headland and began moving leisurely across the little bay, she transferred her attention from the loons to the canoe.

Loon Lake was a peaceful sight, faithfully reflecting the blue sky above, with its occasional small, fleecy clouds floating by, and the trees around the shoreline. There was only one person in the canoe. Pamela tried to decide who it was. He was an elderly man, from the look of him. Yes, he would be at least forty or more, she thought to herself. He was sitting up on the rear thwart, rather than kneeling, she noted disapprovingly. It was obvious, too, from the way he paddled, that he knew nothing about canoes. His strokes were haphazard and clumsy. The canoe proceeded jerkily, in fits and starts, veering frequently this way and that. Pamela's young face took on a more and more critical look. Possibly, she thought to herself, he was visiting with the McKnights. She had heard that they were expecting some friends from Toronto that weekend. Pamela switched her gaze back to the loons. They, however, seemed shy of the approaching canoe. As she watched, they both dived, and look as she would, she could see no further sign of them.

One minute it was a peaceful, quiet and pastoral scene, as far from any possibility of mishap or trouble as could be imagined. The next minute Pamela's heart went into her mouth. The man in the canoe had partially risen to his feet, for some reason, and begun making his way forward. Again, it was obvious that he was not an outdoors person. His movements were too awkward. As Pamela watched, he reached for something in the bottom of the canoe and then turned around. Pamela saw the delicate craft wobble—and the next instant, with a cry of alarm, the man lost his balance and was tipped into the water. Immediately he began thrashing wildly with his arms and shouting for help. It was all too evident that not only was he unable to operate a canoe properly, but he also did not know how to swim.

For a moment, she was too shocked to do anything. Then she looked wildly around. "Judy!" she shouted. "Judy!" But there was no sign of her friend. She looked back at the lake. It was still peaceful and calm: the only difference was—and she knew this for sure—that now a man was drowning in it. Although she was not a good swimmer, Pamela hesitated no longer. She ran down from the little knoll where she had been sitting, and kicking off her sandals, hurried into the water. Her strokes were quick and urgent. She had half-learned the crawl from her mother earlier that summer. It wasn't really a proper crawl—more a cross between a crawl and a dog-paddle—but it soon cut down the distance. Her face slewed quickly from side to side as she kept sucking in breath. She drew close to the man.

He saw her coming and reached out an arm toward her. She tried to swim around behind him. Her thought was to hold him from behind with her left arm, and use her other arm to somehow propel them both back to shore. Suddenly the man grabbed her and she felt herself being pulled down. She fought fiercely to the surface. "Don't grab me," she screamed. "Don't grab me. You've got to relax." Again, she tried to manoeuvre around behind him. But again the panic-stricken man grabbed her and pulled her down.

"Oh God, what am I going to do?" she thought desperately as she struggled once more to the surface. While he was not big he was far stronger than she was. She kicked, pummelled and twisted clear, taking several gasping breaths. The man's eyes, she saw, were glazed with shock; scarcely focussing. To her horror, he raised an arm and struck at her. Fortunately, she was able to avoid the full force of the blow, but it shook her nonetheless. She knew that unless she did something soon they would both drown. But what could she do? There seemed no way to rescue him. She must give up, and save herself. But even as she kicked with her legs, preparing to swim away, she knew she could not do so. She could not let this person drown.

From deep in the core of her being, the invisible wisdom of Mirana flashed through her brain. "Push his head under the water for a few moments," the impulse directed. With a strength beyond her fourteen years, she seized the man by the hair and pushed him under. She felt him struggle feebly, then grow still. Frightened, she let him come up. As his head cleared the surface he began coughing and gasping for air. She knew he was girding up to struggle again, and after a few more calculated moments, she pushed him under once more.

Next time he came up, the man seemed to have lost any impulse to struggle. He yielded easily as Pamela crooked an arm around his chest and looked about her to get her bearings. The canoe, driven by a light breeze that had come up from the south, was already some distance away. Summoning every ounce of resolve, Pamela started to do her best to pull the unfortunate canoeist to shore, using a painfully inadequate backstroke. She felt herself becoming more and more weak. Her arms, legs and whole body ached. She knew she could not keep going much longer. After what seemed like an age, but was in fact a mere four or five minutes, she heard, dimly and through a growing fuzziness in her head, what sounded like a motor. She looked around and saw her father's outboard motorboat. A wave of relief welled up within her as the boat came closer. Strong hands would have lifted her into the boat, but she insisted upon waiting until they had safely retrieved the canoeist. Then she relaxed into her father's arms, sobbing with relief. Her father stroked her head while their neighbour, Dr. Herschel, worked on the man she had rescued. She knew she did not need to worry anymore about *him*. She snuggled her head into her father's lap. She was asleep when they reached the landing of their cottage.

* * *

James Beresford stood with some friends in the shade of an oak and watched his hero crack the ball past second slip for another two runs. Eton's cricket fields basked in warmth as the match between Eton and Winchester approached its climax. With the Eton eleven needing only three runs to win, excitement was high.

"Come on, Hartford-Smith," Beresford thought to himself, for perhaps the fiftieth time. "Come on, give it to 'em!"

Hartford-Smith, tall, good-looking, rugged, looked confidently round the field before taking up position again at the wicket. He was not aware of a youngster called James Beresford. The gulf between the two was something like the gulf between a general and a private. As a member of the prestigious society known as "Pop"—short for "Popular"—the older boy moved at a rarified level symbolized even by the special clothes which he and his fraternity wore.

Hartford-Smith took his usual guard of middle-and-leg and waited for Brown's spin. The ball came curving with deceptive slowness towards him, a little wide. It was a gift. He went for it, hitting it clear over the boundary for a six.

James watched his hero walk in from the wickets with his partner, the applause ringing around them. His heart was close to bursting. He could not have been more excited if he had been a boy in ancient Sparta watching Leonidas return from a victory at the head of his men. His eyes followed the handsome, 18-year-old son of a prominent judge until he disappeared from view. The fact that Hartford-Smith had not noticed him and was unaware of his existence did not bother him. It was enough to have been present! However vicariously, he shared in the glory heaped upon his hero.

He saw Hartford-Smith closer on two other occasions, once as he was hurrying along Keate's Lane on his way to a class, and once when they knocked into each other outside Spottiswoode's Bookshop. At that time he stopped, mouth half open, hardly believing he was so close to his idol. "Sorry," Hartford-Smith said as he brushed past. James tried to think of something clever to say. He enjoyed a role as a leader among his peers, and was not normally at a loss for words. On this occasion, however, none came. Finally he blurted out, "No, really, not at all." But the hero, as he continued on his way, did not hear him anyway.

Two or three weeks later, on a warm Sunday afternoon full of promise, James and a couple of friends went to a favourite spot by the Thames. The air was heavy with the scents of summer. When Thompson and Fowkes remembered a forgotten task and went hurrying back to their boardinghouse, James remained, his face buried in a cricket book. It was his ambition to make the first eleven—perhaps, like Hartford-Smith, to become captain of cricket. A bee buzzed by, checking for pollen, but he scarcely noticed. So engrossed was he in Wilf Rhodes' bowling tips that he did not realize anyone else was near until he heard people talking. One of them sounded familiar, and with a start he recognized the voice of Hartford-Smith. He seemed to be in earnest conversation.

With something akin to panic, James realized that he was an eavesdropper. Should he gather his things together and leave? He was debating the matter when the substance of the conversation became clear to him, and he knew that he could not possibly leave, or even stir a muscle.

"Are you sure no one will find out?" Hartford-Smith said apprehensively. "'Fishy' won't suspect anything?"

"That old fool? Of course not." There was a careless arrogance in the other boy's voice. "Mary left everything just the way it was, so he won't suspect a thing. The exam's in your pocket, old chap. I owed you a favour and here it is, questions, answers, the lot."

James' heart beat so loudly he thought the others must surely hear it. In a low voice, so low he could only just make out the words, Hartford-Smith said, "I've never done anything like this before. But if I don't pass this time my father will never forgive me. What a bind . . . if only I was as good at schoolwork as I am at cricket . . ."

The conversation ceased, and James heard footsteps on the path leading back towards the school. Despite himself, he began to cry. It seemed like a personal betrayal. How could his hero even think of cheating at exams? His eyes were red when he arrived back at his house. He decided to skip supper. He would say he had a stomachache.

It was a week or so later, as he was studying for an exam in history, his least favourite subject, that he too began to think of cheating. "All these darned dates," he thought to himself, "I'll never remember them, not in a month of Sundays." He had been swotting for an hour with very little progress. For some reason he found it difficult to concentrate properly. "You could put a crib sheet in your tails and take a quick look when 'Teapot' isn't looking," he thought. "After all, Hartford-Smith cheats. Why shouldn't you?"

He went over to his cupboard, took out his long black school coat, and examined the two pockets sewn into the tails. Sometimes he and other boys put cherries in one of the pockets, and amused themselves in dull moments by firing off stones at various targets. The overhead lights in the classroom were a favourite. They had curved rims, and if a cherry stone was well flipped it would lodge inside. Yes, he thought. Tomorrow he would put something else besides cherries in his pocket. He would have a crib sheet with him.

He did not sleep well that night. He dreamed he was being pursued by a large yellow lizard with a face like Hartford-Smith. Every time he found a hiding place he heard the lizard snuffling around outside, trying to get in. Off he would run, panting, trying to find another spot to hide. He was glad when he woke up. Bad though this day promised to be, it couldn't be any worse than facing the yellow lizard.

As he walked up Common Lane to his classroom, crib sheet in his tails, he became irresistibly aware of a prompting, as of an inner voice. Magnabaran, his own spiritual reality of being, was saying, *"Don't do it, James. It's not worth it."* The words, inaudible to the ear, nonetheless registered in his heart. He began to have second thoughts. By the time he reached the hallway near his classroom, he had made up his mind. He was not going to be a cheat. He took the crib sheet and flushed it down a toilet before entering the classroom. Once ensconced at his desk he fired off a quick cherry stone, hitting the back of Corky Benson's neck with satisfying accuracy. Poor Corky could scarcely help letting out a yelp of pain and surprise. "Teapot" Tomlinson, sitting at his desk and taking a moment to go over the exam papers before he handed them out, looked up suspiciously. All seemed quiet and orderly, however. Since he was blind as a bat anyway, "Teapot" contented himself with muttering angrily and making vague threats.

Beresford decided it was going to be a good day after all.

Chapter III

1941

Pamela Simpson looked up and said "Thank you" as the maitre d' slid her chair beneath her with practised skill and dazzling smile. The music of the violins added to the feeling of excitement and romance, but Pamela did not need violins to stir such a mood. The excitement and romance was already present, bubbling up from inside. She exchanged a provocative glance with the young member of a Toronto business family who sat opposite her. Pamela's mother was Lebanese, and that had given her a touch—more than a touch—of exoticism. This, combined with her voluptuous figure, caused more than one diner to turn and look discreetly in her direction from time to time.

"What will you have, darling?" asked Peter Burton, looking up from the menu and gazing warmly at her through his horn-rimmed glasses. He squeezed her leg underneath the table, holding it trapped between his own. Pamela felt uncomfortable, without really knowing why. She quietly freed herself.

"I'm so glad to be here again," she said. "I just love the atmosphere of this place."

The waiter came to take their order. They both decided on steak and lobster.

By some kind of tacit agreement they avoided the deeper areas which both knew needed to be discussed. They talked about the Yacht Club and the new boat which Peter and his father had purchased. They got into a spirited discussion about *The Last Tycoon*, F. Scott Fitzgerald's latest book. "Personally, I think he's awful," Peter commented. "His plots are witless and his taste leaves a lot to be desired. But at least he seems to know what he's talking about." They even discussed clothes rationing in Great Britain.

"There are changes coming in the business," said Peter finally, as they lingered over coffee and Italian ice cream. "Dad's feeling his age. He wants me to be the new managing director."

"That's wonderful," said Pamela. Her eyes sparkled with interest. "I think you'd make a marvellous managing director. You've got just the right qualities."

"You think so?" His face lightened perceptibly. "You don't know how good it is to hear you say that. Every now and again I have a few doubts."

"Oh, don't, Peter. Don't. You'll do an excellent job, I know you will. You're intelligent, fair, you like people . . ."

She reached out and placed a hand on his, squeezed it. She felt the confidence rise in him.

He paused, unusually awkward and self-conscious, aware of her hand still lying on top of his. "Pam. Would you like to come to my place after this? We could have a drink and listen to a new Segovia record I've bought."

"I'd love to," she said. What would happen, she was not sure, but she knew that something needed to happen. They had been going together seriously for more than a year now, and in recent months he had begun to hint fairly frequently of his desire to marry her. During her teens, Pamela had never given much thought to marriage. Lately, however, that had changed. Being with Peter was exciting. There was no question he had a good future ahead of him. Life as Mrs. Peter Burton would be safe, comfortable, prosperous, all the things a marriage was supposed to be, wasn't it? Not only that, but she was aware of her own desire increasing. In the past few months, it had taken a lot of self-control to keep herself from giving in to Peter's pressure to go to bed with him. She was a generous person by nature. She increasingly wanted to express that generosity physically.

And yet Pamela was confused. Part of her liked the idea of marriage, but another part of her was not so sure. It was as if a voice within kept telling her that there was more to life than a safe, comfortable marriage with Peter Burton.

His apartment was cosy and tasteful, something he had a knack for. The lights were low, complementing the mellow richness of Segovia's music. Pamela sat down and kicked off her shoes. "Oh Peter," she sighed. "You spoil me."

He gave her a drink. "A new concoction," he said. "Hope you like it." He sat down beside her, a tall, rather gangly man in his early thirties who had never quite been able to extricate himself from his mother's influence.

"Cheers."

"To us." They clinked their glasses.

After a few moments Peter put down his glass, bent towards her and kissed her. She put her own glass down, returned the kiss. Gaining confidence, he parted her lips and their tongues met. He fumbled with the zipper on her creamy silk dress, placed his hand on her soft, warm skin.

She felt again the same intensity that she had known the last few times they were together. A small moan escaped her.

"Darling," said Peter, his voice urgent.

All of a sudden Pamela had a strange feeling as if she was not a part of what was going on. It was almost as if she could see herself and Peter on the chesterfield, as if she was someone separate. With shocking clarity, she realized that she was at a vital moment of decision which would affect all of the rest of her life. To continue on with Peter in this manner would, she was quite sure, lead to marriage. But was that what she really wanted? The voice within her grew more and more insistent. Pamela could not have explained why, but all of a sudden she knew for sure that her destiny lay in another direction. Accepting that, she felt a great sense of relief. She let Peter keep kissing and caressing her, but she was aware, nevertheless, of a merciful cooling in her own level of passion. In a little while she reached out and took one of his hands. Gently, she lifted it away from herself and placed it on the sofa between them.

"Could we have a breather?" She laughed, trying to keep things light. "How about some more music?"

She saw him hesitate. There was a frown on his face. He was a good-natured person though. Obediently, he went over to the record player and turned Segovia over.

He came and sat down beside her again. The machine gave a final click and then began playing. She sensed the feeling of awkwardness between them as they listened to the music. He turned to her.

"Pamela, would you marry me?" he asked, with a slightly lopsided grin.

Here it was, the moment she had been half looking forward to, half dreading. She looked down at her left hand, at the finger where so many of her friends were now proudly wearing their rings.

"I hope it doesn't come as a shock," he went on hurriedly. "This isn't a sudden idea. I've been thinking about it for months. Tonight I knew I just had to ask you."

Feelings raced across Pamela's heart like horses galloping on the range. But somewhere inside her the die had already been cast. She did not know why, but she knew she could not go down the road of marriage with this man. Attractive though the idea was in so many ways, to do so would deny something precious inside herself.

She said nothing for several moments. "Oh Peter," she suddenly exclaimed. She put her arms around his neck and drew him close to her. "Why do I feel the things I feel? Why can't I be normal?" She laughed, a silly, irrelevant laugh, and burst into tears. Her whole body shook. "Part of me would like to say yes but I can't," she sobbed. "I can't, and yet I don't really know why. Isn't that stupid?" She reached for her purse and took out a hanky.

"You just need more time to think about it, Pam." She looked up at him, saw the concern and frustration on his open, uncomplicated face. He released himself from her and went over to the window, looking out at the lights of Toronto. She followed, stood beside him.

"You're a very kind man." She sighed, a long exhalation. She knew what she had to do, what she had to say, hard though it would be.

"I don't think more time will help," she said quietly. "I'm sorry, Peter."

He looked at her dully. "Can I still see you? What's happening, Pam?"

"Let's . . . let's just give things a rest for a bit. Could we, please?"

"Of course, if you want to," he said uncertainly. The feeling of awkwardness was becoming oppressive.

"I think I should be going home," she said. "It was a lovely evening. Thank you, Peter." She gave him a kiss on the cheek.

"I'll drive you home."

"I could take a taxi."

"Don't be silly," he said, impatiently. "Of course I'll take you home."

But they spoke little during the drive to her apartment, and they parted coolly. Only later, as she lay, still clothed, on her bed, the dawn coming through the windows, did she realize what her dominant feeling was. It was one of lightness and freedom. What lay ahead she did not know, but she did not care either. For the first time, she had a delicious feeling of being able to face the unknown. It would even be possible, she thought, to leave Toronto. Perhaps she would go and stay with her friend Christina in Washington, D.C. She decided to go for a walk. The park, with just a handful of early morning runners and walkers, was beautiful. A light breeze riffled the small lake to silver. Pamela walked strongly, swinging her arms and taking deep breaths of the cool, moist air.

* * *

Young Grigori Antoniev had known a strange sense of foreboding ever since he awoke that morning in the farmhouse near the Desna River. Outwardly, everything seemed normal—or as normal as anything can be in time of war. Certainly the Russian sky was normal: a heavy, sodden blanket clung possessively to the stark expanse of snow-covered fields and woods. So was the old building where he and the other soldiers of his squad had spent the night. Even Pyotr Panov's voice, scratchy with age, was comfortingly familiar. But despite these things, and the fact that the nearest fighting was still some miles away, Grigori was aware of a sense of impending doom and disaster so strong that he could scarcely eat the breakfast which Panov's crotchety wife had prepared for them. Alexei kidded him about that, asking him if he was too busy thinking about the flaxen-haired peasant girl whom they had met a few days previously. But no, it wasn't that. It was something new. Something a bit inexplicable—even though he had had his share of being frightened, of being terrified. Who wouldn't, he thought, in the teeth of the savage onslaught by an apparently invincible Nazi war machine?

They sat around the table together, enjoying the luxury of a third cup of tea. Old man Panov, a poor farmer but an experienced and cunning partisan, fondled his hound Tolstoy, dozing on the floor beside him. They had all laughed the previous evening—even Sergeant Mihailovich, who very rarely laughed—when Panov first introduced Tolstoy. Now they had another laugh as the sergeant got up and patted the dog's head.

"So you are called Tolstoy, eh?" the sergeant exclaimed, pulling the dog's ear. His huge shoulders began to shake and once again the great Russian laughed aloud.

"Yes, Tolstoy," Panov exclaimed, delighted to have an audience other than his wife. "As I said to you last night, it is because he loves Tolstoy. Here, let me show you. It will only take a moment." The old man went over to an ancient desk, and after some rummaging returned with a small, tattered book. The way he held the volume and turned the pages spoke eloquently of his love for what was in his hands.

"This is not what most people think in our country anymore. Or perhaps they are afraid, who knows?" he said, with a touch of defiance. "But it is what I think. I will read, and you will see how Tolstoy listens to Tolstoy."

As if on cue the enormous hound got up and sat in front of the old man, head tilted to one side and staring directly at him.

"Tolstoy is writing about the kingdom of God," said Panov. "Listen, please, my friends, just for a moment. 'The only significance of life consists in helping to establish the kingdom of God; and this can be done by means of the acknowledgement and profession of the truth by each one of us . . .'"

As the old partisan continued reading it seemed to Grigori as if the war suddenly ceased to exist. Even his personal sense of coming disaster was forgotten. The sound of distant guns where the Germans were being counterattacked by the First Shock Army faded from his consciousness. A tiny bud of relief sprang open somewhere inside him, and he knew that his eyes were watering. He looked furtively around him, at Alexei, the sergeant, Lev and the others. No one was paying him any attention.

The old man finished reading. The sergeant, whom Grigori had once seen lift a brawny German soldier above his head and fling him to the ground in an unconscious heap, looked awkward. It was Alexei, the scientific, practical one, who spoke:

"He is a fine animal. Has he been trained to run under a tank with explosives on his back? I hear that our mine dogs have been giving a good account of themselves. Many tanks have been destroyed in this way."

Panov fondled the dog's ears. "Tolstoy has been as close to me as a child since our children went away," he said softly. "But yes, he has been trained. Some men of Kopelev's tank regiment came to the village and we put Tolstoy through his paces. He was the quickest and bravest of them all . . ." His voice faltered for a moment. He reached for a photograph that stood on the shelf over the fireplace. "Here. Look," he said, pointing at the picture. His voice was firm again now. "Soldiers of the revolution, and Pyotr Panov in the middle. I was fighting for Russia when you were but a glint in someone's eye. If a chance comes to destroy a tank, we will destroy it, Tolstoy and I."

Pyotr Panov's wife muttered angrily as she disappeared into the kitchen. "This terrible war. Men, women, children, horses, dogs . . . Is nothing to be spared?"

Grigori went and knelt beside the hound, thrusting his hand into the thick grey fur on the back of its neck. "Hello, my friend," he said. The dog turned and looked at him. Brown eyes stared into his own. The creature began to thump its tail.

"Oh-ho," the old man exclaimed with interest. "He does not often do that for strangers."

Outside a whistle blew. There was a sound of running footsteps and shouting. Alexei sprang to the door and pulled it open just as a soldier appeared in the entrance. "A message from the general's observation post, sergeant," the man said excitedly. "They say a German tank patrol may be coming this way."

Sergeant Mihailovich listened calmly, apparently unmoved. Only when the message had been completed did he rise to his feet, buttoning up his battle tunic. He spat into the fireplace.

"Thank you for your hospitality, comrade," he said courteously to Panov. "We must attend to this little matter." He picked up his gun and led the way out of the building.

While the sergeant talked to the lieutenant, the antitank teams took up positions. They had dug "nests" in various key locations to guard the road leading to the village. Vasilii and Grigori had only been together for two months but had already given a good account of themselves. Altogether, Vasilii had destroyed six German tanks in the few months since the panzers began their invasion. Grigori respected him more than anyone else he knew, except his mother and the sergeant.

Corporal Vasilii cradled the stock of the 14.5 mm Simonov antitank rifle in his gloved hands. "The last of a dying breed," he murmured affectionately, sighting along the weapon's slender barrel. "You're not exactly a divisional gun. You are like a peashooter. But it is wonderful what you can do when you are used properly, my little darling."

They lay in their foxhole, the bleak winter landscape of central Russia stretching around them. Grigori had dug the hole carefully, the way he had been trained. A tank could pass over it, hopefully, without crushing them. That was the theory, anyway. They had positioned their gun carefully and checked the ammunitions supply. Now they waited. There was nothing more to do. Either the Germans would come, or they would not. Grigori looked at Vasilii's lean, hard face. "Funny," he thought to himself. "He is the same age as me and yet ten times the soldier that I could ever hope to be."

Grigori was other things. A thinker. A writer. A poet, at times, though God knows he had not written any poetry these past few months. Vasilii was an extrovert, more talkative than Grigori. Sometimes he would talk for what seemed like hours, while Grigori would smile from time to time and make occasional interjections.

But this was not a time for talking. Even Vasilii was silent, brooding as if part of the lonely countryside around them. The cold was intense. Their hands and feet were soon bitterly uncomfortable. Even touching the gun sent something akin to an electric shock through their thick gloves. But it was true, the comment of a German general on the "illimitable capacity" of the Russian soldier for obedience and endurance. And Grigori and Vasilii did not think much about the cold that penetrated their clothing as if it were paper. They thought of their duty to Mother Russia. They thought of the oath they took at the completion of their training to fight to the death. They thought of their girl friends and families. And Grigori thought of Pyotr Panov, who had given him courage by reading a few words from Tolstoy.

Most of all, though, they listened. They had been waiting about an hour when they heard, faintly but unmistakably, the sound which they had been straining to hear. It is a sound no infantryman ever gets used to: the sound of enemy armour approaching. The clattering of tracks and the roar and whine of the panzers' high-powered engines grew louder.

The tanks, six of them, came into view over a small incline. My God, Grigori thought, who would imagine there were human beings inside such evil apparitions? Flesh-and-blood people who perhaps that very day had laughed, told jokes, thought of loved ones and urinated a time or two.

Vasilii fired his first shell at two hundred metres and missed. He swore fiercely to himself and reloaded. The tanks divided, two coming towards Vasilii and Grigori and the rest fanning out toward the other nests. Their tracks grated and tore at the icy earth. The grey turrets turned slowly in search of something to destroy. Grigori saw two tanks take hits. Then with a deafening "whoosh" an enemy shell burst only a few metres from their position. One piece of shrapnel took off the top of Vasilii's head. Another penetrated Grigori's shoulder. He felt his left arm go numb. His head was dazed and he was unable to focus his thoughts. Clods of frozen earth rained upon him. He was totally deaf for many moments, hearing nothing of the din of the battle. Finally his head began to clear sufficiently for him to grasp his weapon, which seemed intact. He peered ahead. A German tank was driving straight towards him, less than fifty metres distant. He had time to fire one round at almost point-blank range, aiming at the driver's port, but the shell missed. He abandoned the gun and desperately threw himself prone at the bottom of the hole.

With a terrible grinding sound, the tank manoeuvred directly over the fragile depression. Grigori squeezed himself next to the body of his dead companion. Nothing in the past weeks or months had prepared him for this. He resigned himself to die. The weight of the monster passing overhead seemed like the weight of a hundred locomotives. He could smell the fumes of diesel. The darkness was like night. Every tremor of the tank's movement reverberated through his flesh. Yet the softness of his body was its salvation: that, and his knowledge of how to dig a foxhole in such a way that a tank could pass over it without crushing him.

The tank moved on a short distance and then stopped. Clearly Grigori heard the gears changing. The tank was going to reverse and back over him, finish him off, he thought. Horror again seized him. Arms, legs, heart, everything, went numb. And in this moment of utter desolation he found himself thinking that perhaps it would not be so bad to die after all. At least the war would then be over, for him as well as Vasilii. Why struggle anymore? Why suffer anymore? What was the point? He shrank back into his hole and waited.

Pirius spoke a sharp command: *"Get up, Grigori. Get moving! You know what you must do. Get up, and run. Now!"*

On impulse, Grigori scrambled out of his hole and, holding his injured arm against his side, began to run for the shelter of the nearby woods. He had been an outstanding runner in his youth. Through his mind flashed a memory of an occasion at school when he had been running in an important competition. That day a wave of applause rang in his ears as he pounded along. Now the sound which bore down upon him and deafened him was the incredible roar of the German tank as it accelerated after him like a predatory animal. At any moment he expected to hear its machine gun spitting death at him. In his haste he put a foot wrong. He tripped, falling heavily to the ground. Pain shot through his wounded arm in agonizing waves. He was unable to raise himself.

Thirty paces away in the trees a small group of partisans put the finishing touches to the harness they had strapped around the dog's back. The fierce-faced old man took the animal's head in his hands and stroked him. "It is time, Tolstoy," he said softly. "Goodbye, my friend." He pointed to the tank bearing down upon the defenceless Grigori. "Tank," he shouted. "Tank. Go, Tolstoy."

Grigori, from where he lay, saw a long grey shape emerge from the woods. The dog flashed past him in the direction of the tank. Even with the load of explosives strapped to his back, Tolstoy was a blur of movement, his long legs and powerful body perfectly synchronized and working to the limit of their capacity. In what seemed like no more than a moment—though it was a moment permanently engraved in Grigori's memory—the creature ran directly underneath the front of the tank. A colossal explosion shook the earth and the air above it as Grigori turned instinctively and buried his face in the snow. Fire swept through the crippled panzer, and he could clearly hear the anguished cries of the men trapped inside. Soon, mercifully, the cries stopped.

The old man helped Grigori to his feet. He looked around him, and saw only the carcasses of burning enemy tanks and a small knot of his comrades hurrying towards him. He tried to speak but no words came. He almost fainted, and would have fallen but Pyotr held him.

"Well done!" exclaimed the sergeant, catching up with them and embracing Grigori and the old man in two mighty arms.

"Grigori led the monster right to us," said the old man.

"I am sorry about Tolstoy," said the sergeant.

Pyotr Panov's face, lined and crevassed by a lifetime of hardship, was stern as granite. A few tears ran down his face. "It is all right," he said, trying to keep his voice steady. "God wished the boy to be spared."

Chapter IV

1941

William Tolliver Kent III yawned, rubbed his eyes, and closed the book which he had been studying. Enough was enough! The radio, which had been supplying quiet background music, was now a medium for some sort of talk. He turned it off. Then, on an impulse, he decided to listen for a moment and turned it back on. So it was that he heard the voice of Colonel William "Wild Bill" Donovan, special envoy of President Roosevelt. He had apparently just returned from a mission to East Europe. Colonel Donovan, shortly to become Major General Donovan, head of the Office of Strategic Services, America's first intelligence agency, was saying, ". . . to study at first hand these great battles going on in the Atlantic and in the Mediterranean, in Africa, in Greece and in Albania. From my observations I have been able to form my conclusions on the basis of full information. These conclusions I will submit to my country for its use in furtherance of our national defence, an essential part of which is our policy of aid to Great Britain.

"We have no choice as to whether or not we will be attacked.

That choice is Hitler's, and he has already made it—not for Europe alone, but for Africa, Asia and the world. Our only choice is to decide whether or not we will resist it. And to choose in time, while resistance is still possible, while others are still alive to stand beside us.

"Let us keep this in mind—Germany is a formidable, a resourceful and a ruthless foe. Do not underrate her . . . . But her greatest gains have been made through fear. Fear of the might of her war machine. So she has played upon that fear, and her recent diplomatic victories are the product. But we must remember that there is a moral force in wars, that in the long run is stronger than any machine. And I say to you, my fellow citizens, all that Mr. Churchill has told you on the resolution and determination and valour and confidence of his people, is true."

Kent switched off the set and got up from his desk. He bunched some pillows together on the bed and stretched out his long, powerful frame into a relaxed position, hands folded comfortably across his stomach. He did not like to exert energy unnecessarily. It was one of life's little ironies that while many of his contemporaries had to huff and puff to keep in shape, Kent maintained a magnificent physique with a minimum outlay of training and exercise. His strength and endurance seemed to come from the outdoors, from long forays in the Maine woods and other wilderness places.

When his roommate came bursting into the room crowing about a beautiful new girl he had met, Kent was quiet. A few words from a man he had never met had stirred something within him, something wild and huge. He did not think his roommate would understand. But he thought Shatner might. He decided to speak to him the next day.

Dean Silas Shatner, Professor of Humanities at McGibbon College, was considered by many to be a crank. Even in New England, home of individualism and self-reliance, he stood out as an eccentric. Probably his height helped. A man who is six feet six inches tall and thin as a garden rake is hard to ignore. Shatner had been at McGibbon as long as anyone could remember, although his time there was but a chapter in a long and varied life that had included ten years teaching in remote parts of China. One thing that no one questioned was his honesty. Daniel Webster might have been thinking of Shatner when he wrote, "The courage of New England is the courage of conscience." Between this man, whose age nobody knew and which was beyond guessing, and William Kent, a strong bond had developed. Perhaps it was because Kent's father, a founder of Kent Industries, had died some years previously, leaving a need in his eldest son's life for someone in whom he could confide. And because Silas Shatner, peering into the clear blue eyes and good-humoured face of his young friend, saw the son he never had.

As it turned out, it was a few days before Kent actually got to speak to Shatner. He had meant to do it right away, but things kept coming up. There was an invitation to a tennis game. A good book he could not put down. One time he stretched out for a five-minute nap after lunch and overslept. When he did find himself with the dean one afternoon, he had almost forgotten the whole business. It all seemed a bit nebulous and unreal anyway. Perhaps nothing more than a mental aberration of some kind. To go off and help fight someone else's war. But the compulsion of Haldan was—in the end—too strong.

"What do you think about the war in Europe, Silas?" he asked. "Do you think we have an obligation?"

The older man's eyes fastened on Kent in the manner of an eagle that has spotted something interesting. He did not speak, however. Kent pressed on. "A lot of people say it's not our business. I guess they figure England doesn't have a chance anyway and we'd be nuts to try to help." He paused, shaking his head. "But I can't agree with that."

"Nor I." Shatner's voice was a decisive rumble from deep in his gaunt frame. "There's something people are missing, William. This upstart little dictator isn't just looking to put Europe in his pocket. He thinks he's a messiah. He's got his eye on us, too, and everyone else. You can count on it."

"You know, when it was debated here at the College, the isolationists won?"

"Damn fools. I'd like to see them debate a squad of panzers." Shatner looked at him shrewdly. He had a knack of going to the crux of things, leaving a person feeling exposed and uncomfortable. "What's on your mind?"

Kent took the plunge. "I happened to have the radio on the

other night and heard a man they call 'Wild Bill' Donovan. He's a special envoy for F.D.R. He was saying that Hitler's Germany operates through fear, but there is a moral force that is stronger than any war machine." Normally Kent's voice was like a summer wind breezing through an orchard. Now it sounded more like a northeaster off Cape Hatteras.

"I'd like to be part of that moral force," he went on. "I'd like to help these guys who are standing up to Hitler. I had a crazy thought that maybe Donovan could use me. I think he's mixed up in a lot of activity behind the scenes. You know, intelligence, espionage, things like that."

"I'm sure he is," said Shatner softly. "'Wild Bill' Donovan. I met him once. A man to match our mountains, as Emerson once said."

"Edwin Markham."

Shatner frowned. "Yeah? Well anyway it's up to you, isn't it, William? A lot of folks would say you're being stupid. They'd say it's not our war. Not yet. And they'd say you only have a year before you major."

"Is that what you think?"

The older man smiled. "No," he said. "It's what I should think, maybe. I've spent a helluva lot of time on you, that's for sure. But you know something, William?" Shatner's grey eyes gleamed. His wide mouth curved downward slightly at the corners. "What use are fancy degrees going to be if we wake up one day and we're not free anymore?"

"So you don't think I'm crazy?" There was relief in Kent's voice. Relief, and something else: a young man's anticipation, perhaps. Shatner smiled. Kent thought he saw a momentary sadness in his fine eyes. "Hell no. Anyway you have to be a bit crazy sometimes. It's an upside-down world. Play it too safe and you never do find out the truth." Incredibly, Kent saw a suspicion of a tear in one eye.

"I'm proud of you, William," said Shatner. He rose up from the chair behind his desk and extended a long, boney appendage, with which he shook Kent's hand. "And now I've got to look after my begonias." Dean Shatner turned abruptly and reached for a small watering can which he kept on a shelf.

Kent felt closer to the old man than he ever had before. He

stood for a moment, watching, as Shatner stooped down to his plants.

"Good-bye, Silas," he said gently. "And thanks." He walked out, closing the door behind him. He knew that a short conversation with an aging and somewhat eccentric Dean of Humanities had changed the course of his life.

Silas Shatner's mind was elsewhere as he went through the motions of watering his plants. He was remembering a young cavalryman who had charged up bloody San Juan Hill in 1898, his long legs driving him ahead of many of the other troopers and the fear churning in his stomach as the cannons roared and bullets whistled around him.

"God be with you, my boy," he muttered to himself. "If I was thirty years younger I'd be with you too."

* * *

It was a cool March morning at the fighter airfield in Sussex, England. Flying Officer James Beresford finished telling about a practical joke which he and some fellow students once pulled on a highly unpopular master at Eton. There were roars of laughter in the dispersal hut, where the men of Flight "A" waited for the order to scramble. They were gathered round a small coal stove which tried valiantly, but quite ineffectively, to bring warmth to the damp, cold building. The waiting, Beresford thought to himself, for the umpteenth time, was the worst part of the whole business. In some ways it was like being in a dentist's office. You knew a call was going to come. The only question was when. Some of the men didn't seem to mind the inactivity. They would doze, or read, quite happily. Beresford's restless, energetic nature was only really happy when he was busy doing something—preferably innovating, trying new ideas, or improving old ones.

Joining the RAF from Eton when the war broke out had itself been extremely innovative. His father, who had been a soldier for most of his life, had nearly had a fit. He'd taken it for granted that his son would join his old regiment. But ever since a distant uncle who had been something of an ace in the previous war had taken him for his first flight when he was no more than eight or nine years old, he had loved flying. It seemed to release something in him, let him explore a new dimension that was free and expansive.

Not that it was all roses. He'd experienced many things since the start of the Battle of Britain that were anything but fun. The times of unutterable fatigue. The hardest times, when a friend was shot up or went missing. The times of sheer panic, like the occasion on one of his first missions when he lost contact with the rest of his squadron and found himself entirely alone, peering desperately out of his fogged-in cockpit, trying to see where death might come from. But beyond all that, there was the sheer enjoyment of flying. More than once he had touched something in himself that was almost mystical in nature. The curious sensation of aloofness and remoteness that only a pilot knows sometimes lifted him to a level of perspective where earthly existence no longer seemed to matter. At such times he felt a sense of peace he had never known before and it took an effort of will to wrench himself back to reality.

The call from the sector controller scrambling A flight came through at three minutes past ten. The small group on readiness alert hurried out of the hut and pounded along the wooden duckwalk as fast as they could in their flying suits and sheepskins.

"Good luck, sir." Andy, the dour, imperturbable Scotsman, offered the word of encouragement as he strapped Beresford into his seat. "Thank you, Andy." He wondered how Andy and the rest of the ground crew felt, fighting the war from the ground, seeing pilots and the planes they cared for getting battered up and often never returning. Then he was rolling down the runway and clearing the perimeter fence. As he reached for the undercarriage retraction lever his engine stopped and missed a few beats before cutting in again. "What the hell . . . ? he asked himself. Turning his head and looking back he saw bombs bursting on the satellite airfield and felt the shock of high explosives. He glimpsed other fighters emerging out of a chaos of black smoke and flying debris. "My God," he said. And then, "Good luck, Andy."

There was no time to think about the devastated field. Those bombs had come from somewhere, Dorniers most likely. He climbed steeply at full throttle and watched the English countryside fall away beneath him. God, how he loved that countryside. He was exhilarated at the thought of action. He and the others caught up with the fleet of Dornier Do 17's and their escort past Pevensey. He gave the first enemy fighter a four-second burst and saw his bullets shattering the hood into fragments that sparkled like leaping droplets of water. The BF 110 rolled over onto its back and fell like a stricken duck, nose first, to the water below. Beresford looked for another target.

"Behind you, No. 3. Behind you, No. 3." Beresford heard Cobber's calm Australian drawl over his RT. He rolled to the left and began turning to meet his attacker, the classic gambit of the fighter pilot. Tracers peppered his starboard wing but he maintained his steep turn. The two planes rushed at each other on a collision course. With a tight feeling in his stomach Beresford knew he was up against a very good pilot. He held his course as long as he dared, finger pressing on his firing button, but at two hundred yards he broke first, pushing the stick hard forward. Under the shock of the negative G his stomach rushed into his mouth and his head cracked on the roof. As he began diving, his Spitfire was hit by a burst of cannon. A sickly smell of fuel began to permeate his cabin. Glancing out of his port window he saw white smoke pouring from one wing.

Beresford turned the nose of his machine toward England, scanning the horizon around him. The sky seemed clear. He concentrated on nursing his machine over the waters of the Channel which, though they sparkled brightly, were bad business for a downed flyer because of the cold and lack of organized air-sea rescue. Now and again the Spitfire coughed and hacked like a smoker with emphysema. Beresford unconsciously tightened his grip on the controls, hanging on like a blind man clinging to the leash of his guide dog, willing the machine to keep going. His eyes continually swept the skies around him for other aircraft, though what he would do if an enemy plane appeared he did not know. There was nothing he could do. He was a lame duck. The proverbial sitting duck. He watched his precious altitude gradually dropping. But he also watched the shores of England drawing closer. Then, as his eyes rotated from starboard to port, he saw a solitary plane approaching on a diagonal course to his own, heading for France. It was some two thousand feet above him. He watched with grim fascination as the plane came closer, then turned and began diving toward him. He could make out very clearly the shape of a Messerschmitt 109. He thought he could also see the two machine guns which the enemy aircraft carried on top of its engine cowling, and the 20 mm cannon on each wing. The muscles in his jaw tightened convulsively. In a voice he would scarcely have recognized as his own, he blurted out, "God, I'm going to be killed."

Erich Wulf, pilot of the approaching Messerschmitt, had had a good morning. In a fight with some Hurricanes over Dover he had added two kills to his already impressive tally of 26 victories. Now, though separated from the rest of his squadron, he headed home with the comforting thought that he still had some reserve fuel and ammunition. Another thought was also comforting him. He was due to be married in a week. Indeed, it took a continual effort to bring his thoughts back from Annette to the realities of the moment. A pilot did not attain Wulf's reputation by day-dreaming. Nonetheless it pleased him to steal the occasional moment—now that he was heading safely home—to picture Annette's warm smile, her dancing brown eyes and her trim waist. They had been sweethearts for more than three years. While she was ready enough, Erich had put off the thought of marriage until that day recently when two close friends ran into trouble over Calais and were shot down. One managed to nurse his machine home, despite severe wounds. The other parachuted into the Channel, never to be heard from again. In the privacy of his room at the base, Erich broke down and wept uncontrollably before the icy reserve of the veteran could reassert itself.

Curiously, though, it was not hate which the loss provoked in him. Rather, it was a new respect for life. While he had it, it must be cherished. He had phoned Annette and his parents, and spoken to the Kommodore of his squadron, all in the same afternoon. And now in just a few days, if life was kind, the two of them would be married.

Suddenly Wulf caught sight of the Spitfire below him. A plume of smoke trailed behind it. With a professional eye, he noted how the machine wobbled, clearly unstable in its handling. His eyes gleamed as he dipped his plane in a sharp, banking turn that would bring him directly behind the stricken British fighter. He steadied his course, made some quick calculations, and put his finger on the firing button. At the same time that he was moving in automatically for a kill, some questions passed through his mind. "I wonder who is in that plane, praying to get home?" he asked himself. "Does he have a sweetheart too, like me?" The Spitfire came directly into his sights. But Erich Wulf had already taken his finger off the firing button. He grinned as he drew alongside the Spitfire and raised a gloved hand in salute. To Beresford's amazement, the German plane flew alongside him for a while, escorting him toward the British coast. Then, with a waggle of its wings, it turned away, climbed steeply and set course once more for France.

The sun, which had been playing hide-and-seek amongst the low-lying cumulus, broke through and flooded Beresford's cockpit with brilliant, intense rays. He closed his eyes for several moments and gave thanks for whatever power seemed to be looking after him. In a few minutes he successfully set the Spitfire down in a field half a mile inland. Unsnapping his harness, he cleared out in record time. He was making his way to a nearby farmhouse when the plane exploded with a tremendous boom that reverberated through the surrounding countryside. An elderly farmer came cautiously down the lane toward him, holding a shotgun in his hands.

"It's all right, old chap," James said, smiling. "I'm on your side. I say, have you got a phone I could use?"

Soon he was sitting in a comfortable chair sipping a strong cup of tea and eating homemade scones. He wished that he could buy the German pilot a beer.

* * *

Pamela picked up the phone and dialed the number of her friend in Washington again. She had been trying for two days, but there had been no answer. Was she on holiday? Sick in hospital? Where could she be? The phone rang once, twice, three times, four times . . . Pamela was just about to hang up when she heard the receiver being lifted off its cradle at the other end. She recognized the voice immediately.

"Hello? Christina here."

"Chris? Hi. This is Pam."

"Pam? For goodness' sake, it's great to hear your voice. How are you?"

"Just fine, thank you."

"I've been thinking about you."

Pam laughed. It was good to hear Christina again. She hesitated, wondering how to say what was on her mind, but Christina beat her to it.

"Do you want to visit?"

Pamela laughed with relief. "How did you guess?" she asked.

"Really?" Christina didn't usually get too excited, but she was excited now. "That's terrific. I'd love to have you. How long can you stay?"

Pamela paused again. She realized she was feeling very emotional. "I'd like to stay a while," she said, trying to keep her voice calm, "if that's all right with you and things work out."

"Of course, darling. Stay as long as you like," Christina said quickly. "Is everything all right?"

"Of course," she answered reassuringly. "I just want to leave Toronto and try something new, like you did."

"Well, you're more than welcome. Gosh, Pam, we'll have a tremendous time."

"I have an uncle in Ottawa. He thinks he could get me a job in our Washington embassy."

"It's only five blocks from where I live. You could walk to work."

"It sounds perfect."

"So how soon can you come?"

"I'm not sure. I have to go for an interview. As soon as I can, I'll let you know."

"Okay, Pam. Take care of yourself."

"I'll get back to you. Bye . . . and thanks."

Pamela hung up. She felt a warm glow inside. Thank God for friends, she thought to herself.

Pamela yawned and put down the magazine she was reading. She might be able to catch a few minutes' sleep before they arrived in Washington. With all the hectic goings-on recently, she could use it. She nestled her head against the pillow. But it was not sleep which came when the lids folded down over her dark brown eyes. It was the memory of the scene at her parents' home when she announced she would not be marrying Peter, and planned to go to the United States.

"Some more rice, Pamela?" her father had asked. He was looking anxiously at his wife. Catherine Simpson's Mediterranean blood was churning and Pamela, her father and her two younger brothers knew it. The eruption came a little later, when her mother spilled some salad dressing on the new tablecloth. Frustration and resentment boiled to the surface. She turned angrily towards Pamela.

"You had such a perfect opportunity to get married," she said fiercely, pointing a finger at her. Neither Pamela nor her father spoke, hoping to ride out the storm. "How could you hope for a better prospect, Pamela? You have thrown away the chance of a lifetime." She was shouting now, her emotions in full control. "Peter has such a good future and he is so kind. Men like that don't come along every day, you know. And this silly idea about going to Washington. Don't you realize you'll be splitting up the family? How can you even think of it?" As suddenly as it had started the storm blew over. Her mother began to cry. Finally, her hands trembling, she resumed her meal.

Her father had been terrific. How she had loved him in those moments, seen him in a different light than before. While he was very successful in business, he had often seemed meek and passive in the face of her mother's powerful temper.

On this occasion, however, he spoke out. Folding his hands carefully in front of him, and looking his wife straight in the eye, he said in a strong voice, "Pamela is a grown woman, Catherine. I'm sure she knows what she is doing. I think we are very fortunate to have such a daughter. She will make someone a fine wife one day. We must have trust." He had turned to Pamela then, tenderness in his eyes, and added, "We wish you well, my dear. It is hard for your mother because you are our only daughter. The important thing is that you feel you are doing the right thing and are happy. That is enough for me."

Tears had come to her own eyes as her father spoke. Through

all the years of her upbringing, his love and affection for her had never faltered. At times, when her mother went on an emotional spree, she had felt sorry for him, knowing his marriage was not always easy. For some reason, though, he had stuck with it, and she knew why. They really did love one another. Now, as her husband spoke, Catherine Simpson looked at him uncertainly. "You think it will work out all right?" she asked quietly, almost like a little girl.

"Yes, I do," her father said firmly. And that was it. Pamela breathed a sigh of relief—along with everyone else—and gave her mother a big hug.

"I love you," she said. They held hands for a few moments until her mother shook her head impatiently and said, "There, there. What's all the fuss about? Get on with your meal before it gets cold."

The train drew slowly to a halt at platform seven and stood snorting and puffing after its exertions. Washington! Pamela felt her blood quicken as she gathered her luggage and joined the other passengers making their way to the exit. She saw Christina waving on the other side of the barrier and smiled excitedly. "Here we go, Pamela," she whispered to herself. "The start of a new adventure."

Chapter V

1944

At eight o'clock in the evening, under cover of the Swiss blackout, two men knocked on the door of 23 Herrengasse in the picturesque medieval section of Berne. An inconspicuous sign on the front door said simply, "Allen W. Dulles, Special Assistant to the American Minister." The door was opened by a kindly, grey-haired man with wire-rimmed glasses and neatly trimmed moustache. "Come in," said Mr. Dulles, who in fact worked for the OSS.

One of the visitors was a middle-aged person of rather portly proportions who looked like a successful businessman. His silver hair was thick and impeccably groomed. His clothes were expensive, and he wore an ornate ring on one finger. But Hans Gruber was not a businessman. He was a senior German government official who travelled to Berne and other neutral capitals at regular intervals on matters involving trade. At 53, Gruber had concealed his dislike for the Fuehrer well. He had done this partly, perhaps, from expediency, but also because he felt the most useful course for him was to continue on in a trusted capacity and fight the Nazis from within. Gruber's companion was a large, athletic-looking young man. Three years' active service with the OSS had toughened William Tolliver Kent III. But his features still carried the same good-humoured expression which—with his other assets—had turned so many feminine heads on the McGibbon campus.

Allen Dulles, an amiable host, ushered his visitors into the living room and poured them a drink. "It is good to see you both," he said. "I hope you had no trouble getting here?"

"No trouble at all," said Gruber, taking out a gold-plated cigarette case and offering it to the others. "Thank you for sending William to meet me." Gruber lit a cigarette for himself, but the others declined. Dulles lit up a pipe, then turned to Kent. "William, did you notice any undue interest in our friend at the station?" he asked.

"Not a thing," Kent replied.

"Good," said Dulles. His tone was affectionate as he turned back to Gruber. "How are things in Berlin, Hans?" he asked.

Gruber blew out a small stream of smoke. He smiled thinly. "Terrible," he said. "You have no idea, Allen, how much suspicion and fear is in the city. No one trusts anyone anymore."

"You must be very careful, my friend. I still think you should accept my offer to help you get out."

The other man shook his head. "No," he said firmly. "I am German and my place is in Germany. In any case there is my family—it would all be too complicated. What does concern me though is that the longer this madman remains in power, the harder we are going to fall." Gruber drained his glass, held it out for a refill. "The sooner an Allied victory occurs the better for us all," he said. "That is why I am here."

There was a pause. Kent looked at Dulles to see if he was going to break the silence, but the spymaster seemed lost in thought. Dulles was thinking back to the first time he came in contact with the German, not directly, but through an intermediary. At that time he had gone through the motions of being interested in what seemed a rather unlikely story. The intermediary, a toymaker from Geneva, had said that a German trade official in good standing with the Nazi hierarchy wanted to feed information to the Allies in order to help bring down

Hitler. Dulles had nodded politely. Said he would be happy to see samples. But he hadn't taken the offer too seriously. When the first batch of microfilm documents arrived, however, he knew that here was the most important contact of his career. Since then the German had provided regular information of very high quality to America and Britain by way of Dulles' base in Switzerland.

"I have a good friend in Italy," Gruber said finally. "He works in a top-secret experimental institute in Milano. It is my understanding that what they are doing has some connection with Hitler's rocket program. In any case, if he can be guaranteed safe passage to America, he would be willing to pass what he knows over to your government."

Gruber looked at the others. He seemed happy with what he saw and he leaned back in his chair with a smile.

"Mind you, I do not know how important my friend's work is," he said. "I have no background in these things. I can make no guarantee. But I do know that both the Germans and Italians keep a close eye on everything. My friend is under constant surveillance."

"How did you communicate?" Kent asked.

Gruber smiled again. "He has a superior who shares his views—our views, should I say? This man was able to have a message sent to me. My friend trusts me to work out the arrangements."

"More schnapps?" Dulles refilled the glasses.

"Why such interest in coming to America?" he asked.

"Ah, there hangs a story. My friend married just before the war. He fell in love with an American tourist. It was soon obvious that it was a mistake—a simple chemical attraction, no more. The lady wanted to return home to America and did so. Then, the war. Then, the news that she had given birth to a son. He knows they will never get together again, but he wants to see his child. He wants to see him badly enough to risk his life, gentlemen."

"It sounds like it will not be easy to rescue this person," Dulles commented.

"No, not easy," said Gruber. "But it could be done. I have a few thoughts, if you would like to hear them."

An hour and ten minutes later Herr Gruber left 23 Herrengasse by the rear door after checking to make sure no one outside was interested in his movements.

The drop point was an alpine meadow about forty kilometres north of Milan. It was Kent's thirteenth operational jump, and it went perfectly. But then, he was not a superstitious sort anyway. He was accompanied by OSS sergeant Frank Gucci, from New York. They landed cleanly and the supplies fell in a tight pattern well within the prescribed area. A motley crew of Garabaldini partisans of all ages gave an enthusiastic welcome to the two Americans. Embraces went on for several minutes, something that embarrassed Kent but did not seem to bother Gucci. Two faces stood out to him: Enrico, the young leader of this band of Communist resistance fighters, and Vincenzo Valpone, the political commissar. Enrico was dark and handsome in the classic Italian manner. He seemed to take to Kent from the moment they first met. Valpone, by contrast, gave the impression of being suspicious or distrustful—even though he chuckled and grinned as he grasped Kent's hand. Valpone was an older man. Kent put his age at around 55. He had learned, through his time with the OSS, to trust his intuitions, and filed his impressions away in his mind for future reference.

His instructions, in the quiet, comfortable flat in Berne, had been to deliver the supplies and spend some time with Enrico's partisans. Next he and Gucci were to proceed with the rescue of the Italian scientist, Luca Frascati, whom they would escort across the frontier into Switzerland. Dulles had stressed that a partisan leader in Milan, code-named Leonardo, would be a key factor in the success or failure of the mission. Leonardo, it seemed, had a cousin who was Frascati's immediate superior in the Posch institute. This man enjoyed the trust of both the Italian and German security people and would act as an intermediary in arranging a suitable rescue plan. It sounded okay in Berne, anyway, Kent thought to himself.

In the latter months of 1944, Italy was a hotbed of political intrigue and infighting. As the tide of war swung increasingly in favour of the Allies, and the joint American and English forces moved northward, Socialist right-wingers, Communists and Conservatives jockeyed endlessly for power and advantage. Supplies of clothes and weapons from the U.S.A. were a life-or-death matter for partisans suffering from attack by the enemy and assault from the elements. OSS policy was to provide assistance on an impartial basis to both pro-Communist and anti-Communist factions, depending upon which could be most effective against the Germans at any given time. However left-wing partisans not infrequently accused the Americans of favouring right-wing guerrillas.

The shipment of sixty automatic weapons that accompanied Kent and Gucci produced a show of intense affection for the Americans. But one evening just four days after the drop, Kent had cause to realize how very delicate their situation was. He and Gucci had gone to visit a nearby village. The way led across a rocky mountain track with horrifying drops and spectacular views of the Alps. During an enormous dinner in their honour, a swarthy peasant with an orange neckerchief got to drinking too heavily. Within Kent's earshot he began boasting to a friend how he and others had buried a cache of arms a kilometre outside the village ready for a Communist liberation movement after the Germans were defeated.

"The Allies will leave soon enough once they have beaten the German pigs," he said loudly. "What will happen to us then? Unless we are ready, Italy will be taken over by another set of fascist swine. The guns must be there when we need them."

Someone muttered a curse and jabbed an elbow into the man's ribs. Kent knew he had heard something that he was not supposed to hear. He pretended not to have noticed. Turning to Valpone, who was on his left, he told a new Mussolini joke which he had heard before leaving Brindisi. The fat commissar laughed heartily, too heartily, Kent thought. He had heard stories about Communist partisans burying weapons, even new American equipment, for what they considered would be an inevitable showdown with right-wing forces. But this was the first on-the-spot verification he had received.

Kent saved his anger, determined to find out more about the arms hidden in the village and other caches. Finally, a few days later, he made a blistering protest to the guerrillas, saying that his country was dropping weapons to the partisans for the purpose of saving American lives. "What you do after the war is your own business," he said. "But I must insist that our weapons be used to fight the Germans. That is why we provide them, for God's sake." He stared challengingly at Valpone and Enrico as he spoke. The latter looked embarrassed. Valpone, however, stood up and banged his fist on the table around which they were sitting. His face was red with anger.

"Who do you think you are?" he shouted. "Telling us what to do? What do you know about our problems? There is another side to this picture, Signor Kent. I advise you to tread more carefully." The commissar stalked out of the meeting, followed by two of his supporters. Kent looked at Enrico. Now the young partisan was not only embarrassed, but worried. He leaned over and whispered quickly in Kent's ear: "I personally agree with what you say. But this is a delicate matter. Valpone is an ambitious and powerful man who does not like to be crossed. You should let this matter rest for now, or there will be big trouble."

Two days later, in a mountain tavern, Valpone took a long swallow and banged his empty glass down on the table. "Maria. More grappa," he bellowed. The woman refilled the glasses and also brought a plate of cold meat. She was good-looking, in a sloppy way. The commissar tried to pinch her bottom but was too slow. He laughed, then leaned forward, heavy arms resting on the cheap, red-and-white checkered tablecloth. His white silk shirt was stained with sweat. He glanced quickly around the room before he continued.

"I have a bad feeling about this American," he said. "You heard him speak out against us. Now I hear that despite my warning he has continued to stir up trouble. I fear he will sabotage our plans."

"I agree with you, comrade," said one of his companions earnestly. He was a thin man whose skill with a knife had won him a reputation as far as Verona and beyond. "His protests are dangerous. We have worked hard preparing our people for the revolutionary struggle that will follow the Germans' defeat.

Our work could go for nothing if the American is allowed to continue."

"That is not all." Another member of the group spoke. "I am afraid that when he returns to his headquarters he will give an unfavourable report of our activities. He may recommend we receive no more shipments."

"We agree on the danger," said Valpone, tapping thoughtfully on the table top. "What are we going to do?"

The thin man extended his forefinger and ran it suggestively across his throat. "There is this way," he said softly.

Valpone shook his head. "It would be too dangerous," he said. "Something more subtle is needed." He cast a watchful eye once more around the tavern. "I hear that Enrico and the Americans will be going to Milano in a few days. They plan to rescue a scientist at the Posch institute and take him out of the country. Now . . . supposing a word were to be spoken to the Gestapo about this event? They would be very interested, no? They would want to take care of this troublesome young American and his colleagues."

"A brilliant idea, comrade!" said the fourth member of the group, the youngest, who had not yet spoken. "No suspicion would attach to us. It would also kill two birds with one stone, I think."

"Yes," said Valpone, smiling broadly. "Two birds with one stone. I like that, Luigi. It is true that I have been disappointed in young Enrico. He is a good fighter, but he is not with us."

"I agree." The thin man spoke. "With Enrico out of the way we will have no trouble finding a more suitable leader."

"Someone who understands what we are trying to do," said the young man, Luigi.

In the corner of the room, behind the small bar, Maria dried the glasses and put them away. She was wondering if Valpone would require her services that night. She thought how nice it would be if he dropped dead sometime. It would mean that one of the younger men would come after her. The way it was, they were all too frightened to be seen with her.

The commissar pushed back his chair from the table. "Very good," he said. "We will proceed with these plans." He turned, beckoned to Maria and squeezed her bottom as she came and stood beside him. "Tonight, Maria mia?" he said, and chuckled as she smiled submissively.

* * *

The girl came over on Hughie's arm and she was gorgeous. Beresford had to admit it. She was lissom, and sparkled with vitality. Her shoulder-length hair shone like a field of wheat in summer sun. A simple green dress with short sleeves and white trim around the neckline showed off her tan, and everything else, to perfection. He stared at her, forgetting his manners. Hugh Trevor-Jones spoke. "Julia, darling, I'd like you to meet a very special friend of mine, James Beresford," he said. "Squadron Leader James Beresford, D.F.C., to do him justice. One of your Battle of Britain heroes, though he won't tell you about it, I'm afraid. James, allow me to introduce Lady Julia Dalrymple." Beresford took her hand and the chemistry was instantaneous. She seemed in no hurry to remove her hand, but returned his gaze with level blue eyes that carried—what was it?—a hint of provocativeness.

"I'm very pleased to meet you, Julia," he said, and he meant it. Two short minutes ago he had been tossing back his fourth martini and wondering if it had been a good idea to come. The party at Hugh's London flat was friendly, but he found it difficult to enter into the swing of it.

Hughie had insisted that he come. He was worried about him, he knew that. Kept on muttering, "James, old boy, you need to marry." Or, "James, we're having a shoot at my uncle's place this weekend. Come along and get away from it all, eh?" With Germany's surrender expected at almost any time, he should have been cheerful enough. Instead he was moody and depressed. He had entered the Royal Air Force with a high sense of purpose, but somewhere along the way things had got fouled up. Was it the desk job they had given him after his crash in 1943? Or the infighting and the jealousy which he observed around him? The shabby treatment given to Dowding and Park had bothered him terribly, but it was more than any of that. He just didn't seem able to forget all the deaths and injuries in his squadron and amongst his friends. Faces and scenes were engraved in his memory and every now and again they surfaced, sometimes in nightmares, sometimes in quiet moments when he was at his desk or riding in a taxi. Oh, what the hell. It was all over, or nearly all over, and here was this girl holding his hand and looking as soft and inviting as a nice, ripe peach. Snap out of it, James, he thought. Be your old self.

Almost reluctantly he let her hand go. "And I'm very pleased to meet you, James," she said. Her voice was soft, with a husky quality that reminded him of Marlene Dietrich. Her eyes held his and she made no effort to disguise her interest. Hughie made an excuse and left.

"What are you drinking?" Beresford asked. They walked over to a punch table. He filled a glass for her and took one himself. "Cheers," he said. "Cheers," she replied. They wandered over to a corner and sat down.

"Is your father Reginald Beresford, the banker?" He nodded, and she went on, "I've met him. I had a summer job at the Tate, and he lent us some pictures for an exhibition."

"Art's a big thing with him," he said. He was looking at her legs. Slim, elegant and sexy as hell, he thought.

"How about you?" she asked.

"Not too much," he laughed. "I like some art. I can't stand this modern stuff, Picasso and what-have-you."

"Not Picasso?" She was laughing too. "You just don't understand him." Her voice softened a fraction. "Perhaps I could help you," she said. He looked at her. There was a definite invitation in her eyes. Suddenly he knew that it was not light conversation which he wanted. He wanted to hold her, feel the warmth and softness of her body close to him. His jaw tensed for a moment as he asked her to dance. They stepped out onto a small hardwood floor where other couples, in close embrace, were dancing to the beat of a foxtrot. She came into his arms as lightly as a feather, and that was how easily she was bowling him over, he thought to himself, but he did not care. He felt animated again. The wide smile which all his friends knew creased his aquiline features. "Good for you, James," said Hugh Trevor-Jones to himself, then returned to a conversation with some elegantly dressed friends.

"Are you still flying, James?" she asked.

"I'm afraid not." A shadow passed over his eyes. "I was in a bit of a crash and they transferred me to a desk job."

"Do you miss it?"

"I don't know." He held her close. "I think I just want to forget it all. A lot of us do."

"I can understand that," she said tenderly. "What do you think you'll do after the war?"

"After the war?" Funny. It still seemed distant, even though everyone reckoned the Germans would give up early in '45. "Banking, I suppose. Dad says he's saving a place for me."

"Levy and Beresford?"

"You've heard of it, eh?" There was the grin again.

"Of course. I'm very impressed. It's a big name in the City."

"Fairly big. Dad's done a wonderful job all through the war, from all accounts."

"You'll have to dress and behave yourself properly." She was teasing him, and he enjoyed it.

"Actually, people think that banking is stuffy, but it really isn't," he said. "Not merchant banking, anyway. You should listen to Dad tell some of his stories."

"What sort of stories?"

"Well, like the time just after the Russian revolution when he was sent to Russia to open up some trade. He had all kinds of official backing but the Bolsheviks got suspicious and tried to put him in gaol. He escaped by canoe through the Polish lakes—with God knows how much money hidden in his socks."

"I hope his socks didn't have holes in them."

He looked at her, pretending to be pained.

"I'm sorry. It really is an interesting story. Actually I've always thought of merchant bankers as rather a special breed."

"Mind you, it's changing," he said, a note of regret in his voice. "Things are going to be a lot more regulated after the war. The old days of empire-building are gone forever, I'm afraid."

"I'm sure you'll enjoy it," she said. Her cheek rested gently against his. Her words caressed him like a physical touch. He felt his desire increase.

"Julia," he said, almost inaudibly, nuzzling her ear.

"Yes, James?" Still the hint of provocativeness.

"I was wondering if you'd like some fresh air. We could walk to the river—it's very close to here."

"I'd love to."

They thanked their host and left the party. The moon was nearly full, lighting the dark waters of the Thames with a silvery radiance. They stood, for a moment, gazing at the water, then as if by mutual agreement turned and kissed. The kiss was long and deep. She put a hand around his neck, drawing him closer. They kissed with increasing urgency.

* * *

The wall began to glow with a soft, violet light and those present in the room became silent. The hush deepened in intensity and now the wall gave the impression of being alive, almost as if a person could see through it. It looked as if a sheet of crystal glass were in the background, with a dusklike darkness back of it and a moving screen of light in front of it.

"Welcome," said Lord Perakleos, to those gathered in the conference chamber, "as we give specific consideration and enfoldment to the movement of our creative plan on earth.

"I am particularly anxious to bring you up to date concerning Prince Tauhelion, who, as you know, is coordinating our work there at this time, being incarnate as a doctor by the name of Lionel Denton.

"If you look at the screen now, you will see a picture of Dr. Denton at work in his hospital, cleaning some of his instruments. Here is a person of remarkable integrity. You will notice the care with which he attends to even the smallest details. Since an initial spiritual awakening which occurred when he attended the 1936 Olympic Games in Berlin, he has been moving consistently and strongly in an increasing experience of oneness with his true being, Tauhelion.

"Many human beings who have a spiritual experience of some kind tend to become self-satisfied and think that they are illumined. They do not realize that they have merely touched the outer fringe of the realm of light. Fortunately, this courageous man is too humble and honest for that. He knows that there is more to experience and understand—more changes to be allowed to occur in himself—and he is

simply concerned to keep expressing a genuine quality of character in his living. He has no pretensions to personal glory or recognition, and indeed, his nature is such that he would be very happy simply to go his own way in quietness and peace. His integrity, however, impels him to a greater acceptance of personal responsibility both for himself and his world.

"I am now moving to England to show you a few pictures of Prince Tauhelion's consort Princess Sorah-el, who as Elizabeth Waring will become Denton's wife, we trust. The cycle is already in motion—though they are no more than acquaintances as yet in the outer sense—and should come to fruition at about the same time that Denton finally recognizes his true source and identity as Tauhelion, and his absolute responsibility for what is occurring on earth. As you can see from these images, Elizabeth is a warm, outgoing woman who, though she is younger than Denton, has been moving strongly in the direction of the truth for several years. No doubt her unhappy marriage has been a helpful factor in this. She and her husband, by the way, will be undergoing divorce proceedings quite soon, thus opening the way for a closer connection to be made between herself and Lionel Denton."

Lord Perakleos paused, allowing space for stillness in the room. When he spoke again, it was with a certain note of seriousness, even gravity, in his words.

"Now to some less happy matters," he said. "The bitter struggle known as the Second World War continues to be waged on planet Earth, wreaking suffering and havoc to an unprecedented degree in human experience. For purposes of enfoldment and radiation, we will share for a few moments in an overview of various aspects of this conflict, brought to us on the screen. I would point out that terrible and destructive though this foolishness is, and, of course, totally and utterly unnecessary, it may nevertheless be used to advantage in the fulfilment of our creative purposes on earth. The upheavals that are occurring are so massive in their scope, and in their effect on people, that inevitably there will be a breaking down of many of the crystallized traditions and beliefs that have tended to hold human beings in bondage. The opportunity for awakening will, in other words, be flung wide open to all who have the integrity and common sense to take it."

Once again, Lord Perakleos paused. There appeared on the screen a series of pictures showing various heads of state closeted with their advisers; white-smocked scientists and research workers busy in their laboratories and institutes; army engineers busy constructing testing sites; and other images all characterized by an almost frenetic level of activity.

Perakleos spoke again, his voice even more etched with sadness. "These images comprise probably the most damning indictment of humankind that could be imagined," he went on. "What you see is our creation actively seeking to develop nuclear weapons to obliterate one another. It is only a matter of time before they develop this means for total self-destruction. This emphasizes that we do not have unlimited time at our disposal. Nor, of course, does humankind. A sufficient number of men and women of integrity must be found who will allow our plan of restoration to take effect while there is yet time."

Chapter VI

1944

Sergeant Yuri Mihailovich was a formidable man at any time. When he was angry he was very formidable. He was now very, very angry.

The young German girl—she could not have been more than nine or ten years old—lay on the bed screaming and sobbing, her thin immature body half-naked and her clothes dishevelled. Beside her, arrested in his work, was the corpulent Russian counterintelligence officer known, behind his back, as Boris the Butcher. He stared in surprise at the sergeant and snarled, "Go away. Leave us alone." When the huge sergeant did not leave, Boris slowly climbed off the bed and stood beside it, putting his trousers on and trying to project as much authority as was possible in the circumstances. "I said leave us alone," he snapped. "Immediately. I will then overlook this intrusion."

No doubt that would have been the wise thing to do. The expedient thing. It was not good to make an enemy of SMERSH. It was better to tread softly with them, even though one might despise these well-fed policemen who avoided the rigors of the front, doing their dirty work behind the lines while keeping their eyes open for valuable booty.

Mihailovich didn't always do the wise, expedient thing, however. As he looked at the young girl cowering against the wall, trying to cover herself, the man who a few days before had led a charge on a German machine-gun post once again threw expediency to the winds. Raping German women in and of itself, and even shooting them afterwards, was not unusual. It happened every day as the advancing Soviets pushed savagely across the Polish border into Germany. Now, as he stared angrily across the room, every part of Yuri Mihailovich's being revolted at the inhumanity of the man known as Boris the Butcher. He clenched his fists and moved closer. Speaking softly but with the menace of an angry grizzly, he said, "Leave the young girl alone or I will break every bone in your body."

Now Boris was under pressure. Expediency was something he was good at, however. If his skin was in danger, his rule of thumb was to do whatever was necessary to preserve it and then, with time at his disposal, figure out a suitable response later. Eyeing the sergeant's formidable fists and the muscles that bulged under his simple soldier's tunic, Boris concluded that a soft answer would be the most prudent course. Later—well, later, things would be different. He even managed a smile.

"As a matter of fact I was just leaving anyway," he said, throwing in a throaty chuckle. "I have tired of the girl." He finished pulling on his clothes and went to the door. Before leaving, he turned and eyed the sergeant, who was comforting the girl. "You will be hearing from me, Sergeant Mihailovich," he said, his anger coming to the surface despite himself.

A few minutes later some of Yuri's men came into the room. "What is happening?" asked Alexei, staring at the unfamiliar sight of his sergeant holding a small girl on his lap and swaying gently from side to side. He was singing a few words of a lullaby which his mother used to sing to him as a boy on the farm in the Ukraine.

"That swine Boris was here," the sergeant rumbled, breaking out of his lullaby for a moment. "War is a bad business and we have all done things we are not proud about. But this . . ." He held the girl more tightly in his arms. "This is inexcusable."

Alexei looked worried. "Did you say Boris?" he asked. "He passed us as we were coming in. He looked very angry. He is not a good man to have as an enemy."

"It's true. I have heard some bad stories." It was Rashinsky, the sniper, who spoke.

Sergeant Mihailovich set the girl down on the bed and stood to his full six feet three inches.

"I am sure they are all true," he growled. "But I have not come this far in this war to be frightened by a fat SMERSH bully who attacks ten-year-old girls. Come. We must go. The girl's grandmother is hiding upstairs and will take care of her." He bent down, and awkwardly, formally, shook the girl's hand. "You will be all right now," he said gently. "Good-bye, little one."

The men left the house, which was situated in a small town near the Polish-German border. From an upstairs window an elderly, grey-haired woman peered after them, then left the window and hurried downstairs. An ugly red welt covered one of her cheeks. Boris had struck her as she tried to protect her granddaughter.

They took the sergeant away on a phony charge the next morning. The brigade commander had made a muted protest—"You realize this man is one of my best sergeants?" But he was not going to stick his neck out for Mihailovich. Nor was anyone else. As the sergeant was led off to a waiting car, with the sound of heavy guns booming not far off, only one man was moved enough to do something. And that was senior lieutenant Grigori Antoniev, a hardened warrior of the First Shock Army. In a few moments the sergeant would be gone, perhaps forever. It was not really a conscious decision on Grigori's part which set his strong legs in pursuit of the sergeant and the small convoy of SMERSH men accompanying him.

"Sergeant Mihailovich," he called. "Sergeant Mihailovich."

The sergeant and his captors stopped. Grigori came to a halt a few feet from them. What pushed him forward in this manner? The same impulse which caused British and German soldiers in the First World War to sometimes forget their conflict for a few moments and exchange cigarettes, jokes, friendship? It should have been a normal enough thing to wish to say good-bye to his own sergeant. But he felt as if he was crossing a thin, delicate line, with an invisible chasm on the other side. Having taken the step he had, though, he was in no mood to turn back, no matter how many threatening looks the men from SMERSH gave him.

The captain of counterintelligence spoke. "It is not permitted to speak with the prisoner. Be about your business." He was small and tough, with a hard, white face. He did not raise his voice. As a senior NKVD man, he did not need to. He had done it all and seen it all, and the things he had done, many of them hard and inhuman, gave his voice authority. As the officer stared at him with cold eyes, Grigori felt a ripple of fear move through him. But he did not yield.

"He is my sergeant," he said simply. "I wished to say good-bye to him."

In a moment the sergeant had moved out of the group and the two embraced.

"I heard what you did," said Grigori. "It was the right thing. I wanted to tell you. Good-bye, I wish you well."

They stood together on a little patch of snow-covered soil in Germany.

"Who is this soldier?" the small captain snapped angrily.

A regular officer spoke up. "This is Lieutenant Antoniev," he said. "He is in the same company as the sergeant."

"I want him brought along also," said the captain. "I will question them both. Tell the brigade commander."

The officer hurried away.

"Quickly. Move," said the SMERSH captain, pushing Sergeant Yuri Mihailovich. The dumbfounded Grigori was also shepherded along by counterintelligence men who carried automatic pistols.

Such a thing could not be happening, he thought. People do not do this to their own countrymen. What was the sense in taking good fighting men from the front and sending them to prison or interrogation or whatever it was they had in mind?

But it was happening.

Then the sergeant turned back and winked and Grigori knew he had no regrets. He would follow his instinct. He had known this kind of impulse before.

"If you can follow this man into the teeth of German machine guns and trust him you can follow him into this cat's cradle," he thought to himself. He winked back at the sergeant.

As they half climbed and were half pushed into the waiting car he thought of the time the sergeant had saved his life near the Furtsova bridge on the Don.

He had been trying to repair a small lorry, working underneath it, when the jack slipped and he was pinned to the ground. The sergeant heard his shouts and raced to the scene. Such strength seemed impossible, but setting his legs strongly beneath him, the sergeant lifted the front of the vehicle a few inches while other men feverishly pulled Grigori clear. Afterwards, for fun, three of them tried lifting the vehicle. They were unable to budge it. "My God, but he is a strong one," Rashinsky had said in awe.

* * *

They stood on the roof of Milan cathedral looking out over the Lombardy plains.

"It is like a beautiful garden, Signor Gucci, is it not?" The middle-aged partisan leader beamed with pride. His jolly face seemed to drink in the panorama around him, for Leonardo loved the rows of mulberry bushes and poplar trees which divided the greenery of the plain into little squares. To the east, the plain stretched in an unbroken vista as far as they could see, to Venice and the Adriatic. On the southern side the view ended in the Apennines, running from Bologna to Genoa. To the west and north lay the Alps, with the peaks of Monte Visto, Monte Rosa and the Saasgrat rising majestically to the skies.

"Yeah, nice," said Gucci, without too much enthusiasm. He was not a great one for scenery. He wondered when the exuberant, moustachioed partisan would get down to business.

"The distance from the pavement to the top of this cathedral tower is 356 feet," said Leonardo. "After St. Peter's at Rome and the cathedral of Seville, this is the largest church in Europe. It can hold 40,000 people."

"Yeah?" Gucci was 25, recruited by an OSS staffer in New York. He was smart, tough and streetwise. He was also Italian to the last drop of his blood. Gucci had been born in Sicily and brought to New York by his uncle, a noted mafioso who became his guardian when his father was slain in a fracas on the Palermo waterfront. Gucci was seventeen when a vengeful dope dealer drew a revolver and tried to blow his uncle's brains out. Without conscious premeditation he had dived for the man's legs and brought him down. It was a little enough thing but it had strengthened the bond between himself and his guardian. Some thought that he might one day inherit his uncle's authority. That didn't weigh too much with Gucci. He wasn't even sure that he wanted to be an active member of the family forever. He took things very much as they came. Perhaps that was why he listened with interest when one of Donovan's men, an attorney who had met Gucci in the course of a business dealing, told him about OSS work.

Gucci saw Leonardo looking at him expectantly. He thought he should try to appear interested. "What's that white thing?" he asked, pointing to a building about twenty or thirty kilometres south of the city.

"Ah, that," said Leonardo. He was obviously pleased. Gucci braced himself for another lecture. "That is the Certosa of Pavia, one of the most magnificent monasteries in the world. It was begun in 1396, ten years after the first stones were laid for this cathedral. However, most of the Certosa was built in the fifteenth century. It is without doubt the finest example of Renaissance architecture in existence."

"Yeah? You don't say." Gucci figured he had paid his dues. He looked about him. He saw nothing suspicious.

"Can we talk about Frascati?" he asked casually.

"Ah yes." The partisan leader's lips turned down at the corners of his mouth and his usual good-natured expression faded for a moment. Gucci thought that jovial though he might appear, he was doubtless well capable of slipping a knife into someone's back. Hopefully a German's.

"We have some bad news," he said finally. "Our scientist friend thinks he is being watched more closely. The outer arrangements are the same, but he has this feeling that something has changed. One thing he has noticed is that he has a new guard, a Gestapo man by the name of Reiner. We know him. He is not a nice man at all."

"So?" Gucci's jaw edged forward aggressively.

"It's just that Signor Frascati is a sensitive man. If his suspicions are correct, well . . . it may mean there has been a leak," Leonardo continued. "These are difficult days in our country. There are so many groups and they all have their special interests. Betrayal is common, even though we all have the same enemy."

"So you think Fritz may be on to us?"

"It's possible, signor. I do not know. Perhaps the security people are simply getting more nervous."

Gucci's jaw advanced another millimetre. "I'm not losing any sleep over it. What's the plan, Leonardo?"

Leonardo's eyes crinkled. "Patience, my young friend. We are still working on some details. Bring Major Kent to my house tomorrow evening at seven o'clock, and we will discuss them."

They walked down the long, spiralling staircase leading from the roof to the ground. At the bottom, Leonardo turned. "The roof is supported by 52 pillars with canopied niches for statues," he said. "And do you know how many statues the cathedral has?" Leonardo paused, waiting for an answer. "No fewer than 4,440, signor! Think of it." Gucci tried to look impressed.

"I wonder if they are coming?"

Enrico voiced the thought in the minds of them all. He had been peering through the window of the Milan apartment toward the church of Saint Ambrogio for half an hour, and was getting stiff. "Leonardo, take over here, will you?" he asked. Leonardo soon saw what they had been waiting for. A large black limousine drew up at the entrance to the historic church. The chauffeur climbed out first, looking carefully around him. He was followed by the scientist, Frascati, and a third man.

"Jesus, would you look at him!" said Kent. He was studying the scene over Leonardo's shoulder. "Who let him out of the zoo?"

Leonardo laughed shortly. "That is Reiner. I could tell you some interesting stories about him. He likes to kill people with his bare hands."

"The smaller one must be Bohm," Kent went on. "It's what we expected. Bohm will stay outside with the car. Reiner is going inside with Frascati. Everything looks okay. Let's go, you guys—and watch your ass."

Enrico was a few steps behind the large American as he left the apartment. He was grinning as he whispered to Leonardo. "Do you think he ever gets nervous?" Leonardo grinned back. "I doubt it. But let's see."

Gucci slipped into the church first. He was glad that Leonardo was not with him. The partisan would have gone on for five minutes, telling him about the ancient wooden door with its carvings of scenes from the life of David. Fortunately Leonardo was stationed outside, ready to deal with the chauffeur when the time came. Gucci dipped his fingers in the holy water and crossed himself. As he walked down the aisle, his footsteps echoed loudly. He took a pew near Reiner. The plainclothesman looked around briefly but didn't seem too interested in him. From time to time Reiner glanced at a nearby confessional. That was where Frascati would be baring his soul to the priest. Looking at the tremendous width of Reiner's shoulders, Gucci could believe all that Leonardo had said about him. Ah well, he thought to himself. If all went according to plan the bastard would soon be lying on the cold stone floor with a dart from Gucci's tranquilizer gun in his neck. Gucci had wanted to use the throwing knife which he carried strapped to his right ankle. He was good with it, and it seemed the obvious way to him. But Kent insisted on the OSS gadget. "Just as effective, but no mess," he had said firmly.

Kent, dressed in a monk's habit, sat across the aisle in another pew counting his rosary and praying with great diligence. Even though low murmurings and occasional chanting drifted in from another part of the church, the room was very quiet. Kent, who was not a churchgoer, felt oppressed by the heavy, musty smell. What would Silas Shatner think, he wondered, if he could see him now? He wanted to laugh, but that would not fit with the image he was cultivating at present.

The plan that had been worked out was very simple. As soon as the scientist emerged from the confessional, Gucci would deal with Reiner and escort Frascati out of the church, with Kent bringing up the rear. No one would try to stop them. Ordinary people did not look for trouble, and indeed, it might be supposed that the Gestapo man had simply fainted or fallen ill. Outside,

Leonardo would have taken care of the Gestapo chauffeur, and with Enrico driving, the four would make their getaway in Enrico's van. They planned to switch vehicles before driving north to Lake Maggiore, which they would cross by small boat, hiking on foot through the mountains into Switzerland. "The Germans are keeping a close watch at the border these days, so take care," Dulles had warned.

Suddenly there was the sound of shooting just outside the entrance to the church. Looking around, Kent and Gucci saw a uniformed Gestapo officer hurrying forward, accompanied by a squad of soldiers. Gucci reached instinctively for the little dart gun in his shoulder holster, but even as he did so a huge hand clamped on his arm like a vice and twisted it violently behind his back. Reiner chuckled in his ear. "One more move and I will break your arm," he said. At the same time the officer and his troopers formed a tight semicircle around Kent. The Gestapo captain was young, slim, good-looking. He smiled, showing white teeth. "Major Kent, I believe? We have been expecting you. Please give me your weapons." Kent looked at Gucci, immobilized by Reiner. He looked at the soldiers. There was no choice. Slowly, he brought out his revolver and gave it to the German. "Danke. By the way, my name is Woller. Captain Woller."

Enrico, keeping watch outside the church from his van, had seen Leonardo cross the street to deal with the German chauffeur. The plan was that he would engage him in conversation and then deliver one of his favourite karate-style chops to the neck. The two men began to talk. Suddenly, the Gestapo man drew a revolver. Enrico watched, horrified, as Leonardo tried to grab the gun. A shot rang out, and the partisan fell to the ground just as a German military vehicle squealed around the corner and disgorged a load of soldiers at the entrance to the church. The Germans disappeared into the church, to emerge minutes later with Kent, Gucci, and Frascati. Both car and lorry drove off in the direction of the Gestapo headquarters. It had been a nice setup, Enrico thought to himself bitterly. Obviously Frascati's vague fears that the Germans suspected something had been well-founded. Enrico started up his van and drove off. There was a lot to do. The contingency plan was a gamble, but it was all they had now.

"Were you surprised to see us?"

The young Gestapo captain sat back in the comfortably padded leather chair in his office and studied Kent, who, with his hood removed, looked a most unlikely monk indeed. Two armed guards stood by the door. Reiner sat in a chair in a corner of the room. Although he was not holding a weapon, Kent thought he looked the most intimidating of the lot.

"I was indeed," Kent replied. "It wasn't really in our plans."

Woller laughed, a little smirk of self-satisfaction creasing his face.

Gucci, sitting in a chair beside Kent, leaned forward. "How did you know?" he asked, his face friendly. Fast as a viper for all his bulk, Reiner sprang across the room and hit Gucci with his open hand. The blow knocked him off his chair and hurled him to the floor. Reiner smiled. "If you don't mind, we will ask the questions," he said. "All right?" Gucci wiped some blood away from his face. He made no reply. He wasn't sure he could have spoken even if he had wanted to. His black eyes stared intently at the man who had struck him. He smiled back, as best he could, and clambered back onto his chair. The one bright spot in this whole charade, he thought, was that when they searched him they missed the knife nestled behind his right ankle. His fingers itched to seize the slim pearl handle.

"Sergeant Reiner. I am conducting this investigation." Woller did not stir from his chair or raise his voice, but his words cut across the room like a knife. Only a muscle twitching at the side of his jaw told of the anger he was holding in check. That, and the intensity of the gaze he turned upon the SS sergeant. Kent thought that while Woller might be young, he had plenty of guts. Reiner seemed to have a certain respect for his superior also. He mumbled something and sat down again. His hands rested like sledgehammers on his knees, a jagged white scar clearly visible across the back of one of them.

The building which the Gestapo had taken over for their Milan headquarters was a four-storey house formerly belonging to a banker. The room where they were now closeted was spacious and elegant, with sumptuous curtains and chandeliers and a high ceiling. Large portraits of Hitler and Mussolini hung above Woller's head. The house stood on a quiet boulevard that had been built by the Spanish in the sixteenth century.

Woller turned to Kent. "How well do you know Signor Frascati?" he asked quietly. "Are you friendly with him?"

It was a delicate question. If the Gestapo wished, they could easily take Frascati apart and find out where his loyalties lay and whether he had been a party to the rescue attempt. But they might not wish to do that. They might wish to keep him as healthy—and happy—as possible until he finished his project.

"Not really," said Kent. "Someone heard about his work and thought it would be smart if we could get our hands on him and find out more about it, that's all. By the way, where is he?"

Woller ignored the question. "So he did not collaborate with you in this ill-fated venture?" he asked. He picked up a silver-plated letter opener and tapped it idly on his large, ornate desk. Kent saw in one corner a photograph of the captain with a flaxen-haired young woman and two small children.

"Hell no," Kent replied. "This was all our own idea. He didn't know a thing. We wanted it that way—less chance of a leak."

"How did you know he would be coming to confession at Saint Ambrogio this morning?"

Kent smiled knowingly. "That wasn't difficult," he said. "We have been keeping watch on his movements."

"I do not believe you," said Woller calmly. "No doubt you have friends both inside the Posch plant and outside. I want to know who those people are, Major Kent. And what other activities you have been engaged in."

"May I ask you something?" Kent said casually, almost as if he had not heard. "How did you know we would try to get him?"

Reiner half rose.

"One moment, Reiner." Woller waved a hand. "I will humour our friend for a few more moments." He smiled confidentially. "We didn't, really. Our information was not specific. We knew the possibilities, that's all. It was unlikely that you would try a direct assault on the villa—so well guarded, as you must know. We have discouraged other interests of Signor Frascati, but confession and mass are two things he insists upon and we allow him these little indulgences."

Woller paused. His voice hardened. "Now, Major," he said coldly. "The information, please. There is no need for any unpleasantness. But if I have to use Reiner, then I will do so."

He's been playing with us, but he is not going to play anymore, Kent thought. The big question was, how Enrico was doing. How soon would he be able to mount their contingency plan? An armed rescue attempt against the Gestapo HQ was a perilous venture but with the increasing confusion and loss of morale caused by Allied victories, it was by no means impractical. Kent decided there was nothing to lose in playing for time.

"Any chance of some coffee?" he asked.

To his surprise, the Gestapo man snapped his fingers. One of the soldiers left the room, returning shortly with a tray bearing a pot of espresso, some cups, and a plate of biscuits.

"Please. Help yourselves, gentlemen," said Woller, eyes fastened on the American. "As I say, we try to be civilized."

"Danke schön!" said Kent. The strong, scalding coffee rasped its way down his throat. As he opened his mouth to speak again, an explosion shook the room.

"What the devil?" Captain Woller was on his feet. He shouted to his men, "Outside, see what is going on." As they jerked open the door and dashed outside, Gucci lifted his pant leg with one hand and grabbed his weapon with the other. The slim throwing knife flew swiftly across the room and caught Reiner in the throat. The Gestapo man gagged, fell to the floor, arms and legs thrashing. In the same instant Kent's fist landed cleanly on the side of Woller's jaw. His head snapped back and he sagged awkwardly into his chair. "Sorry," said Kent. "But at least you'll wake up, which is more than our friend Reiner will." He unsnapped the holster at Woller's belt and took the pistol. Gucci paused for a moment and wiped his knife on Reiner's shirt. "Come on," shouted Kent. Outside there was the sound of firing and more explosions as hand grenades went off.

As the two men fled they heard Enrico's voice shouting, "Major Kent! Major Kent!" An SS man heard Kent and Gucci coming and turned toward them, raising his machine gun. Gucci's hand flicked forward and the man collapsed, blood spewing from his throat. In a single, flowing motion Gucci picked up his knife and the dead man's gun. The two hurried on.

"Hurry! To the courtyard—we already have Frascati," Enrico cried. Enrico and the partisans maintained a vicious fire as they retreated to the entrance, where a black van waited, its engine running. There were shots and shouts behind them. "Ahh . . ." said Gucci, and fell suddenly. Kent paused, looked at him. "My leg," said Gucci, "I can't move. Go on." Bullets spattered around Kent as he scooped the injured man up into his arms and ran to the van.

The partisan at the wheel revved the motor. "Enrico, come quickly," he cried, while Kent also shouted, "Enrico!" With a last burst of automatic fire the young partisan leader turned and ran towards the vehicle. He was six feet away when a uniformed SS man brought a rifle to his shoulder and fired. The bullet hit Enrico in the back. For a fraction of a minute he stood still, triumph turning to dismay. He fell to the pavement. The driver cursed fiercely and stamped on the accelerator. Kent saw Enrico make a feeble attempt to raise himself. He collapsed and lay still. "Dammit to hell," the American muttered savagely.

As the van moved forward and gathered speed down the street, Kent reached out and pulled the front door shut. He turned, looked into the back of the van. The scientist was checking Gucci's leg. He looked up at Kent. "He was lucky," he said. "It is a clean wound. The bullet went straight through the calf." As he spoke, Frascati tore a strip off his shirt and applied a bandage to the bleeding leg.

"Thanks," said Gucci, his face etched with pain.

"It is the least I can do," said the scientist solemnly.

The van had turned into a maze of small side streets. Soon it was parked out of sight in a dilapidated garage. The occupants transferred to a small grey Fiat saloon, which left immediately, slipping through the city's northern outskirts on the Saronno road minutes before police roadblocks were set up.

Chapter VII

1945

Like a funeral column, the prisoners moved across the bleak expanse of snow-covered steppe. The warning of the Chief Guard had long since died out on the freezing Arctic air: "Attention prisoners. On the way to the work site you will keep close column. Hands behind your back. One step to the right or one step to the left will be considered an attempt to escape, and the convoy will shoot without warning. Remember, one step to the right, or one to the left."

A bitter wind whipped up the thin skiff of snow that had fallen a night or two previously, cutting visibility to a few yards. Head down, hands behind his back as the regulations demanded, Grigori trudged ahead, his feet following the feet of the man in front. There was no talking on a morning like this. Every ounce of energy was needed for survival: keeping one's feet on course and handling the awful cold. It was only three kilometres to the construction site, but in this cold it seemed to take an eternity.

There was not a tree to be seen anywhere. The wind blew untrammelled from the frozen caps of the Arctic and mocked the small band of men that laboured doggedly along the ill-defined road. Guards with rifles and warm sheepskin coats were strung along each side of the marching prisoners. Normally they would shout periodic warnings and instructions to the prisoners but on this morning the shouts were few. Apart from the hiss of the wind and the shuffle of feet in the snow, the silence was total.

Grigori found himself thinking of Sergeant Mihailovich, who had fallen foul of an NKVD captain and been put in a punishment cell. Grigori was worried about his friend. He had been acting erratically lately. Sometimes he would become irritable and lash out at someone without warning. At other times Grigori would see him sitting alone, brooding. When Grigori tried to cheer him up it sometimes worked for a little while. The sergeant would seem to recapture something of his old spirit as long as Grigori was with him. But he would slip into depression again, once he was on his own.

They were about half a kilometre from the site when Burdsev the Lithuanian packed it in. Whether he simply decided he had had enough, or whether he lost his orientation, Grigori never learned. All he knew was that there was a sudden commotion ahead. He heard shouting, and then the ominous crack of a rifle split the air, swallowed almost immediately by the stillness. The men, however, kept moving. Passing by the spot where Burdsev had broken ranks, Grigori saw his tall, skinny frame stretched out in the snow, two soldiers standing beside it. The snow was red in places. One of the guards shouted at Grigori to face to the front and keep moving. Well, he didn't mind doing that. It meant someone else was going to have the job of bringing the body in. Would anyone miss Burdsev? Grigori wondered as he trudged on. Probably not. He was unmarried. No one would give him a thought. Well, you weren't the first, and you won't be the last, Grigori thought to himself. He remembered a time the previous week when the Lithuanian had brought him half his ration of bread because Grigori was sick and needed extra nourishment.

Burdsev had been what the world would call a "loser." Ill-equipped, either physically or mentally, to stand up for himself, he had been a constant target of jokes and annoyances, some harmless, some not so harmless. Grigori and Sergeant Mihailovich had done their best to make life a little easier for him. One time, when another prisoner tipped over the ladder that Burdsev was climbing, the sergeant came to his defence, smashing the prisoner to the ground with his fist. But basically Burdsev did not have the will necessary to survive in a place like Ust-Ulenov. And so, Grigori thought wearily, perhaps what had happened was not only inevitable but kind. No more suffering for Burdsev. No more humiliation.

That evening, Grigori returned to his hut to find the new camp lieutenant waiting for him. The lieutenant had decided to conduct a surprise search and found a knife hidden in a corner of Grigori's mattress. The knife had been given to him just two weeks before by a former navy man, Volstok. It had been a labour of love on Volstok's part, fashioned with infinite care out of a piece of steel slipped to him by a friend who worked in the foundry. With the knife, Volstok had been in a position to perform useful tasks for prisoners in return for which he received various benefits. When a boulder dislodged and fell on him in the rock quarry, crushing his chest, Volstok knew he would have no further use for the knife. And he certainly wasn't going to see it go to waste. So he had told his friend Grigori—while Grigori held his hand and tried to comfort him—that the knife was his. Grigori had thanked him, and he died with a look of contentment on his face. Grigori retrieved the knife later from its hiding place in Volstok's mattress, and hid it in his own.

When the lieutenant saw Grigori's reaction to his discovery, a smile of self-satisfaction flitted for a moment across his face. His vigilance had been rewarded. "Oho, what have we here?" he said, displaying the knife. "What have you to say about this, Antoniev?"

Grigori said nothing. There wasn't anything to say. Finally, after ranting on about how serious the matter was, the lieutenant took Grigori aside. Lowering his voice, and fixing him with a crafty conspiratorial gaze, the lieutenant said he would be prepared to be lenient with him, even though he was a disgusting criminal, if Grigori, in return, would provide a little friendly cooperation.

"What do you mean?" Grigori asked, though he had a pretty good idea what the lieutenant had in mind. "What sort of cooperation?"

"Nothing very much," said the lieutenant. "Sometimes things

go on in the camp which we need to know about, that's all. You could be a big help to us, Antoniev."

"You want me to be a stoolie?"

"I wouldn't put it like that." The lieutenant was still friendly. "It's in everyone's best interests if we can stop trouble and keep things orderly. You must realize that."

"Get someone else to do your dirty work," said Grigori emphatically. Whereupon the lieutenant's smile quickly disappeared and the full weight of his authority made itself felt. Grigori was sentenced to ten days in the punishment cell.

Ten days in the punishment cell at Ust-Ulenov corrective camp proved a death sentence for many. For others, the starvation ration and continuous cold aggravated ill health and set up problems which would remain with a man all his life. Grigori began his sentence with no illusions as to his situation. He knew he would be fortunate to come out of this alive. He was young, which was one point in his favour. He also had a good constitution. The trouble was that he was already weakened from a chronic and debilitating diarrhea.

The food ration was 300 grams of bread per day, with a little gruel every three days. There was no window in the cell. The floor was bare cement. The stone walls were covered most of the time with a thin layer of ice. True, there was a small stove, but it was lit very infrequently and only for the purpose of melting the ice off the walls. This, of course, caused pools of water to gather on the floor. At night, he slept on the bare boards.

On the evening of the fifth day, Grigori ate the last crumbs of his bread and curled himself up on the boards with the single grey blanket clutched tightly around him. He put a hand on his ribs and was shocked at how thin he had become, and how cold his body was. There seemed to be no heat left in it. From somewhere in the same block an awful groaning noise began. It went on for several minutes before Grigori heard the heavy feet of a guard pass his cell door. The groan changed to a scream and then stopped abruptly. Grigori's thoughts returned to himself. A sense of despair welled up within him. As the cold pressed in he began to wonder if he would survive another night. The cell was like a living tomb. He thought of getting up and walking around a few times to try to get his circulation going. But he did not think he even had the strength to do that. "Grigori, my boy," he thought to himself, "you are in a bad way." He realized that part of him rather liked the idea of dying. Part of him wanted to give up, and let the cold have its way. It would be a merciful trip into oblivion. Why not? he asked himself. But another voice told him that he must live, that there was a purpose to his life beyond anything that he had yet known.

Somewhere deep inside himself Grigori yielded. He did not give in to despair. He yielded to a powerful living force within. He yielded to the same force which had brought a friend back to life after a forty-day illness which should have killed him. Yes, he thought weakly, many amazing miracles have occurred in the camps. He wondered if he would be one of them.

Fully prepared to die, he was also at last willing to live. More than that, he sensed the rightness of being allowed to live and fulfil his destiny. Grigori relaxed, and as he relaxed he became aware of a strange inner warmth that seemed to come from another world. It infused his body with new life and hope. "All is well," he said to himself, and went to sleep.

When he awoke he felt more rested than he had for days, even weeks past. The guard was Ryuskin, who tried to make things a bit easier for the prisoners. Ryuskin banged on his cell door and pushed his plate of food through. There was a ration of gruel. He was not due gruel until tomorrow. The guard winked at him. "Thank you, Ryuskin," he said. And to himself he said, "You're going to make it, Grigori Antoniev."

* * *

The embassy Christmas party was a nice affair, not too quiet but not too noisy either. Ambassador Tweeton, a large, vigorous man who once played football for McGill, took Pamela aside at one point and told her how pleased he was with her work in the documentation section. Several of the male staff flocked around her, which was nothing unusual, and took advantage of the opportunity of kissing her underneath the mistletoe. Pamela was friendly, but did not feel her usual lively self.

Christina drove her home, stopping the car outside Pamela's house on H Street. "Gosh, I'm glad I didn't have that last drink Rick tried to push on me," she said with a laugh. "Any coffee in your place? It might perk me up." They walked up the steps of the old brick house. Pamela had recently redecorated her room. She had bought a new painting, and covered the gloomy walls with an interesting combination of wallpapers. A plush wine rug replaced the rather worn and colourless carpeting that had been there for thirty years or more.

Christina picked up a little bronze Rodin. "You haven't lost your talent for decorating, Pam," she said. "May I make myself at home?" She flung herself down on the bed with a comfortable sigh and looked up at the ceiling reflectively. Pamela went to the kitchenette to make coffee. "Glad you like it," she called out. "I'm surprised how quickly it went. I only started the wallpapering on Wednesday." She emerged a few minutes later with a tray and two cups of steaming coffee. They sipped in silence for a few moments. Christina eyed Pamela over the rim of her cup.

"Could I ask you something, Pam?" Her voice was casual, but Pamela sensed an underlying concern.

"Of course."

"It's not really my business. But is something bothering you?"

Pamela opened her mouth to answer and then hesitated. There were some things that one felt shy about bringing up with anyone. The silence continued for several moments. Christina made no effort to break it, but just looked at her friend. A smile crinkled her wide mouth. Christina was fair, lean-limbed, and made Pamela think of canoes and mountaineering. She was also honest, sensible and affectionate—the best friend anyone could wish for, Pamela thought to herself.

Pamela smiled ruefully and shook her head.

"I don't know," she said finally. "I'm just a bit confused, I guess."

"Is it anything particular?"

"Yes and no," said Pamela. "Look, I don't want to bore you, Chris."

"Don't worry about that," her friend said.

"Well, remember how I told you once I nearly got married in Toronto?"

"You mean Peter Burton? The one who was just about to take over the family business?"

"That's right. Everybody thought it would be a perfect match. Except me."

Christina laughed, a happy, wholesome laugh that helped drain some of the tension from Pamela.

"Are you having second thoughts, Pam?" she asked.

Pamela laughed herself. "No," she said. "Not about that. But you're right, Chris. I guess something has been bothering me. You see, I left Toronto with a feeling that something big and exciting was going to happen. I didn't know what, but . . ."

"It hasn't happened?"

Pamela laughed again, and let out a deep sigh. She felt better already, just being able to talk about it. "That's right. It hasn't happened . . . and sometimes I wonder if it ever will happen. Or if it was all just imagination or something."

Christina put down her coffee cup and leaned forward, hands clasped around her knees.

"Don't give up on your dream," she said softly. "Call it a woman's intuition, or what you will, but I believe in it. There is something big in you, Pam, and it will find its own way to come out."

Pamela walked over to the cocktail cabinet and brought out a bottle of wine and two stemmed glasses. "I've been saving this for a special occasion," she said, smiling. "I think this is it. Let's make a toast, Christina. To the future!"

"To the future," said Christina.

They raised their glasses, their eyes meeting in silent affirmation.

* * *

It was a memorable day for Reverend Jeremy Brown, vicar of Saint John's church in Higher Woodicombe, Buckinghamshire. There had not been such a flutter in the little parish for years. Saint John's had been the family church of the Dalrymples for many generations, so it was only to be expected that the wedding would occur within its venerable walls. Lady Penelope had come down several times to look at the inside of the church—as if she did not know it, down to the last ancient beam—and to check the arrangements. "It will be perfect, Jeremy, just perfect," she said finally. She laid an aristocratic hand on his arm, winked and added, "Perhaps it's time you thought about getting married." Reverend Brown, a middle-aged man whose wife had left him ten years previously to run off with a soldier, turned deep red. But inside he was pleased that she thought him young enough to marry again.

The day itself dawned clear, blue and sunny. The Chilterns had never looked more beautiful. Riding on his ancient bicycle with the basket in front, Reverend Brown was everywhere, attending to last-minute details. Eyes beaming behind his thick glasses, he even stopped the church groundskeeper on the high street and asked him anxiously, "Did you cut the grass this morning, Bert?" The old man was clearly upset. He growled, "Why don't you go and have a look, Vicar?"

Reverend Brown had a light lunch with his housekeeper and then hurried down to the church. My, what a large and elegant congregation there was! Lords and ladies. Dukes and duchesses. Dowagers. Elegant young men and women of substance—and, of course, RAF friends of the groom. They kept crowding into the church so that for the first time in many a long year it began to be really full. Reverend Brown reflected wistfully that it would be nice if the church was filled like this all the time. But he had stopped worrying about that long ago. He usually comforted himself with the thought that "You can lead a horse to water, but you can't make him drink."

The hymns resounded magnificently within the old Norman walls. Reverend Brown read one of his favourite passages, Paul's discourse on charity, and gave, he believed, one of his finest renditions. Then they moved on to the nub of the matter in which everyone was most interested. "James," said Reverend Brown in his most solemn tone, "wilt thou have this woman to be thy wedded wife, to live together according to God's ordinance in the holy estate of matrimony? Wilt thou love her, comfort her, honour and keep her, in sickness and in health; and, forsaking all others, keep thee only unto her, so long as you both shall live?"

James Beresford felt a sudden wave of uneasiness. A sense of uncertainty. He remembered how a sense of doubt had obtruded into his consciousness a number of times during the past few months, to be quickly repressed and pushed aside. It was so much fun being with Julia. He enjoyed her friendship and her physical charms so much.

"For God's sake get on with it, James." His best man, Squadron Leader Peter Smith, D.F.C., did not say the words aloud. But he thought them with such intensity that he was almost afraid he had.

"I will," said Beresford, at which little shivers of sentiment ran up the spines of the young women present, and some older ones too. Reverend Brown turned to Julia and put the same question to her, except that she was also asked to acknowledge her willingness to obey her husband.

"Who giveth this woman to be married to this man?" the minister asked, at which cue Lord Dalrymple stood, a fine figure of a man at any time, but all the more so in his splendid, formal attire. "I do," he said gruffly, jowls quivering.

"Isn't she beautiful?" a gorgeous young woman whispered to her boyfriend as the couple took their vows. The young man nodded politely, but he was thinking back to his own experience as Julia's lover. "All the best, James," he said silently. "By God, you'll need it."

Chapter VIII

1948

The steamship Orion moved majestically into New York harbour, tugs fussing around her like courtiers welcoming a returning monarch. She gave two imperious blasts on her horn just in case anyone was unaware of her presence.

Forty-three-year-old Dr. Lionel Denton stood forward on the starboard side looking at the welcoming arms of the Statue of Liberty and thought that it was good to be home—even though his fiancée was still back in England. He had spent a week visiting with Elizabeth Waring and her family and making plans for the wedding which was to be held at the end of the year.

Denton was a handsome man with dark, slightly unruly hair, an athletic build and a direct, penetrating gaze. During the return crossing from Europe, several people had tried to strike up an acquaintance with him, but while he was always pleasant and polite, he had proven to be strangely uncommunicative. It was not that he did not like people—far from it. But during the voyage home he had been concentrating his energies on a project of such vast dimensions that no one on the ship could have understood it. It had begun during the 1936 summer Olympics in Berlin. As he watched great athletes from many nations give expression to their love for sport—and their respect for each other in their quest for excellence—he had sensed a spirit that transcended human ideologies. Hitler's great ambitions seemed to shrink to nothingness as Jesse Owens tapped a hidden reserve of that spirit, propelling his smooth black body to gold after gold. This spirit, Denton realized, was universal. It included all creation within its scope.

What had begun with the Olympics expanded during World War Two. He spent much of the time as a medic in one of the largest trauma units in the Pacific, yet he emerged from the war convinced of the healing, integrative power of life in even the most difficult and horrifying circumstances. He became aware that his own love of life seemed to hasten the healing of his patients. He sensed a restorative force moving easily through him.

The war came to a conclusion. But Lionel Denton continued, day in and day out, week in and week out, to give primary importance to expressing a transcendent quality of character in his living—the same quality that he had first touched when he was at Berlin in 1936. He wanted to prove to himself if such expression, such an orientation, could deal effectively with the challenges of life. The more he moved in such a way, the more he knew that the answer was "yes." Here was the answer—and, as far as he could see, the only answer—to the awful problems which he saw multiplying everywhere in human experience.

His recent visit in England with his fiancée, an attractive divorcée named Elizabeth Waring, somehow confirmed many things in his consciousness. No sooner had the Orion set sail from Southampton for New York than he began deliberately to write down on paper some of the thoughts and principles which he had been developing these past years. All across the Atlantic he wrote, and thought, and wrote. Very little effort was involved, for the words seemed to flow as naturally and easily as from a spring. In this way the mind and heart of Lionel Denton became consciously aware of the wisdom of a source which had seemed for a long time to be beyond himself but which he now realized was himself. The experience brought with it a profound sense of responsibility. It was unthinkable to keep unspoken the truth he had become aware of. It was to be shared, offered freely to the rest of the planet. He had a task before him greater than any he could possibly have imagined.

As the gangplank was moved into position, Denton's thoughts went back to the time when he first touched a sensing of another world. As a young medical student he had gone to hear the New York Philharmonic Orchestra. Toward the close of the concert he found himself buoyed up by a sense of peace so strong that he forgot his surroundings. It was so real and wonderful that he was disappointed when the concert finished. As he walked out of the concert hall and looked at the people around him, all busy chattering, he wanted to say to them, "Don't you realize this is not the real world? There is another place. Can't you hear it? Can't you hear the sweet silence?" What he had touched did not last, but the memory of it did . . . and the determination to find the source of that transcendent experience.

"At last," Denton thought to himself, as he stepped once more onto American soil, "I have found that source."

* * *

The hotel was small and comfortable. The weather was magnificent. The Mediterranean, like liquid turquoise, sparkled a short distance from their bedroom window. After lunch Beresford stretched out in a deck chair near the bar, idly scanning the harbour for sailboats. What an ideal setting it was, he thought, to tap a new spring, to let something fresh flow into his marriage.

It needed it, that was for sure. Even choosing a hotel had led to a quarrel, with Julia wanting to stay in a large, expensive place full of elegant cocktail lounges and shops and lots of men who would stare and smile and open doors for her and generally feed her vanity which damn well did not need feeding. He had stuck fast to his argument, however, that they needed a quiet place where they could relax and simply be alone together.

He believed he had finally been able to touch a chord of agreement in her. Would it hold? His wife, he had long ago realized, was inconstant in more ways than one. That she had a weakness for men in general had soon become painfully obvious. But even more than that, the trouble was that Julia lacked staying power—or was it stability? She was not a cruel or unkind person by nature. But it was a fact that she hurt people—she had hurt him—because no one could predict how she would behave at any particular time. Just because she was interested in something or someone one day did not mean that that would be the case two days, or a week, later. A new stimulus would come into her life and she would give her responsive interest and attention to that.

He saw his wife stepping lightly toward him. She wore a yellow cotton sun dress and a floppy straw hat with flowers and a wide brim. Her long hair was golden in the sunlight and she was radiant. No other word for it, Beresford thought to himself, as he watched her approach. He felt a fierce tug in his heart, remembering when they first met and the promise that he had felt at that time. It was still capable of tantalizing him.

"Darling, you look gorgeous," he said, and gave her hand a squeeze as she sat down beside him.

"Did I ever tell you you've got a superb chest?" she asked playfully.

Beresford smiled and ordered drinks for them both.

"Now what do you think of that for a view?" he said.

They sipped their drinks, to all outward appearances a young, good-looking, happy couple enjoying their holiday.

Julia stole a sidelong glance at her husband. "I'm sorry we had a fight on the plane."

"So am I," said Beresford. He was still looking at the water. "It seems like we've had a lot of fights lately."

"I'm sure we can mend things," said Julia pliantly. He was aware of her hand on his bare arm; her fingers caressed his forearm with soft strokes like an artist's paintbrush. The desire he had felt so strongly that first night they met, and which was still present despite all the arguments and fights, rose up in him again. He looked at his wife, enjoying the way her breasts molded the thin fabric of her dress, the way her lips parted slightly.

"Let's go upstairs," she said. "Too much of this heat can be dangerous, they say."

She looked at him, her fingers tightening on his arm. He hesitated. He knew something needed to be resolved between them, to be honestly brought into the open. But how to go about it?

"Julia, I've been thinking . . ." he began, and then stopped. It was so hard to start. So hard to express what was in his heart.

"What is it, darling?" she asked, everything about her alluring. "Come on, darling, we can talk in bed if you want to."

God, he thought, how much he wanted this woman. True, they needed to let down their defences, come clean with each other, and share what was happening beneath the surface. But if he pushed too hard there would be another fight. Maybe he should just forget it, he thought. Perhaps this time, as they made love, they would finally dissolve the barriers that had been growing between them. Her fingers tightened on his shirt sleeve, pulling him from his chair. He let himself be pulled.

* * *

By early afternoon it was over one hundred degrees in the middle of the Siberian summer. The bags of cement had to be passed from the supply wagon to the area where Gang 12 was working on the new mess hall. It was a distance of about seventy-five metres, but it might have been seventy-five kilometres. After working for a little less than an hour Andropovich knew that he was not going to last much longer. He had been feeling weak for several days, ever since the boil developed on his back. It was bad luck, he thought, that Zavrenov had chosen to keep an eye on the work. Zavrenov was a terror to the prisoners, a guard who enjoyed violence. On this particular afternoon he seemed to be in an even worse temper than usual, shouting and hurling abuse for no reason at all.

By contrast, Andropovich, the camp philosopher, was a gentle man of fifty or so years who was liked by almost everybody. Nearly all of the camp's inmates at one time or another had found comfort in talking with Andropovich. And it wasn't mere philosophical theory that he handed out. He lived as he taught, never condemning anyone, always suggesting, in his quiet, unassuming way, a rational approach to trouble.

Like automatons, the prisoners kept the heavy bags moving from man to man. Grigori, standing next to Andropovich, passed the bags to him with great care. Andropovich, in turn, passed them on to Gorelov, the sturdy Georgian, who swung them as easily as if they were filled with feathers. A little further down the line Yuri Mihailovich, the former army sergeant, still a large and powerful man despite his four years in the camps, maintained a smooth and easy rhythm. Zavrenov walked up and down checking the movement of the bags. The sun became hotter. Shortly before mid-afternoon Andropovich tried to take a step toward the waiting Gorelov but with the cement still clasped to his breast spun around and collapsed on the hard ground. As the human chain ground to a halt, shouts and questions began to erupt from some of the gang members. The gang leader ran up to investigate. Zavrenov and two other guards also hurried to the spot.

"What's going on here? Stand aside," Zavrenov bellowed. He had unslung his rifle from his shoulder and used it to knock one prisoner out of his way. Seeing Andropovich on the ground, trying to get up, he scowled with rage and kicked the fallen man in the ribs. "Get to work," he shouted, "or it will be the cells for you." He kicked Andropovich again. With a desperate effort the philosopher pulled himself to his feet, looking around with half-focussed eyes. "It will be all right," the gang leader said excitedly to the guards. "See, he's all right now."

White-faced, Grigori stared at Zavrenov and tried to still the fury in his heart. He wanted to throw himself at the guard, but even as the impulse sent tremors through his body he knew that he must keep calm and not be foolish. He squeezed his fists together so tightly that the nails bit into his flesh, then deliberately took a deep breath and exhaled slowly. A feeling of peace pervaded his mind and body as the breath moved out, the same inner peace that he had first known in his freezing cell a year or so previously. With it came a sense of power, as if no one could hurt him or make him lose his balance. His heart filled with compassion for Andropovich but in the clarity of mind that accompanied the sense of calm he knew that no useful purpose would be served by objecting to the guards' brutal treatment. Indeed, any attempt to interfere or resist would make things worse. He was also keenly aware of the larger sense of purpose that had been quietly blossoming and unfolding in his mind in recent months.

At first his idea had had no real definition, no clear-cut shape.

It was a feeling, nothing more. A feeling that he had a mission to perform that reached far beyond the confines of Ust-Ulenov—indeed, beyond even the confines of Mother Russia. But then one night, as he lay awake, things came into focus. He would write a book. He wanted to share his life—his friendships, his insights, the terrible hardships of the camp—with the world. How else to do it but through a book? What better way to do it? He had no pen or paper, but that night he composed the first two pages in his mind. When he had finished, he went over the pages, committing them to memory. He went to sleep with a profound feeling of excitement moving through him. He was no longer a pawn in a cruel system. He was no longer prisoner No. 511 in a bleak spot near the icecaps of the Arctic. He was a free man with an important mission.

Sergeant Yuri Mihailovich, a Hero of the Soviet Union until they tore off his shoulder boards in Germany, watched Zavrenov's boot thud into Andropovich. His dark eyes flickered. Once those eyes had been filled with courage and authority. But over the past year or so his spirit had seemed to burn low, and a veil was lowering itself across his eyes. He still worked well. He was handling the stresses of camp life physically. But as Andropovich said to Grigori one night, shaking his head with a worried frown, "The sergeant has no sense of purpose." Free time was a rare commodity in the camp, but the two spent as much time as possible with the sergeant, drawing him into conversation and, whenever possible—although rarely—into laughter.

Now, as the sun beat down upon the little group of men near the mess hall, Sergeant Mihailovich stepped out of the line of prisoners. He walked with long, unhurried strides up to the three guards. A smile lit his drawn, rugged face—as each prisoner who witnessed the event would later recount. Were the guards too startled to react? Perhaps merely curious, wondering what the sergeant wanted? Or were they a little in awe of the inexplicable? For certainly there was something strangely impressive and foreboding about the huge man who approached them.

One of the guards unslung his burp gun and held it, uncertainly, at his side. Zavrenov still held the rifle with which he had clubbed a prisoner out of his path. The sergeant stopped two or three feet from Zavrenov. His voice was clear and authoritative, neither loud nor soft. "You are an insult to humanity," he said. As the guard tried to bring his rifle up, the sergeant raised an arm like a small oak tree and struck Zavrenov a terrible blow on the side of his neck. The guard wilted. His face turned white. Clutching his throat, he crumpled to the ground. There was a burst of fire and the sergeant staggered, his body torn nearly in half by the bullets. He sprawled across the body of Zavrenov.

A growl of rage rose from the prisoners. The guards, looking shocked and frightened, raised their guns threateningly. "Stand back," they shouted. "Back. Keep your distance." A whistle blew and more guards came running. At their head was an NKVD officer, Major Sarolansky. Sarolansky was a fair man. He had fought in the war too. He shouted at the guards, "No more shooting." Sarolansky bent down and examined Zavrenov and the sergeant, then stood up, shaking his head. "Kuznetkin," he called. As the gang leader approached, the NKVD man said, "There will be an enquiry, of course. But we must not make it worse than it is. Put your men back to work."

Kuznetkin nodded. He spoke urgently. "One of my men, Andropovich here, is ill. He is too weak for this work. He needs to see the doctor."

Sarolansky pursed his lips. "Of course, Kuznetkin," he replied. "Send him along." He turned to the guards. "Get busy and remove these bodies," he snapped. The guards looked startled. Normally such a task fell to the prisoners. They went to fetch a wagon while the prisoners too went to work, the bags of cement once more moving in a chain.

"Good-bye, Sergeant," Grigori said softly to himself, passing a bag to Gorelov. The guards loaded the bodies of the two dead men onto a cart under the watchful eyes of the major. At Ust-Ulenov, where the death rate was two or three per day, the incident would soon be forgotten. But Grigori had it in mind that the sergeant would never be forgotten. He had decided what he would call his book. It would be entitled *Sergeant Mihailovich.* He wrote another three pages that night, oblivious of the bedbugs that crawled over him.

* * *

Abraham Lincoln sat in his great marble chair staring out upon the world with unseeing eyes. Below, a small handful of visitors gazed up at him in awe. At least, some gazed in awe. Not the very tall old gentleman who stood chatting with a young friend a few feet away from where Pamela was standing. They were an unusual pair, and from time to time Pamela stole a quick glance at them. The elderly one, she thought, looked a bit like Lincoln. He had a somewhat similar beard and he was just as gnarled. He reminded her of the hickory cane which her grandfather had favoured; he was a hickory cane with clothes on it, she chuckled to herself. The man's companion was large, fair, and about her own age. Pamela looked at him with interest, sorry that she could only catch a partial view of his face from the side. Beside the older man he did not look particularly tall, but she guessed he must be over six feet. There was something about this younger man that intrigued her. She put it down to his evident strength and good looks.

"People respect and appreciate him now," said Silas Shatner sharply. "But do you think they did when he was alive?" A few heads turned in his direction. "Not on your life," said Shatner, grinning wickedly. "He was too honest. Made people uncomfortable. I'll tell you something else. The Gettysburg address was a flop. It went over like a lead balloon."

"Wet blanket," said the young man. "He told friends later that it went over like a wet blanket."

"Hmph." Shatner frowned slightly.

Intrigued by the older man's comments, Pamela looked in his direction. Suddenly his companion turned and glanced at her. She felt a strange sense of disturbance. Why did this large young man with the look of a Daniel Boone or Davy Crockett seem so familiar? She looked for a long moment at the fair-haired giant standing a few feet from her, and he looked directly at her. She thought she had never seen such striking blue eyes. She would have liked to smile or say something, but how could she? It would not be proper, she thought nervously. In the same instant something of the same thought passed through the mind of William Tolliver Kent III. It was one thing to tangle with the Gestapo, to blow up an enemy supply depot in Greece or fasten a mine to a German cruiser in Taranto Bay. But to respond suitably to this unexpected situation seemed beyond his ability. The impulse of the spirit battled with the constraints of convention—and lost. They both looked away.

However, recently retired Professor Silas Shatner was not bound by conventional behaviour. At some indeterminate point in his long and colourful life he had decided that it was an unnecessary burden. And so he delighted in saying what he thought, when he thought it—or in being quiet, if that was what moved him. Shatner's silences, and of course his caustic comments, disconcerted a lot of people, but those who looked beyond his outer ways found a man of gold. Shatner looked up at Lincoln and began a quiet oration to his companion.

"The dogmas of the quiet past are inadequate to the stormy present . . . . We must think anew and act anew. We must disenthrall ourselves . . . ." Though he spoke the words unobtrusively, the rich timbre of his voice carried them clearly to Pamela. Perhaps he sensed her interest, had noted her presence near him. He turned to her, a smile softening the stern lines of his craggy face and said, "Excuse me, young lady. But I was brought up on the words of Abraham Lincoln."

A blush crept into Pamela's cheeks. "Let us have faith that right makes might," she replied. Her smile lit the whole surroundings, as far as Kent was concerned. "I'm a Canadian but I've always felt he belonged to all countries," she said.

"Hmph. Canadian, eh?" said Shatner, his deep-set grey eyes appraising her with evident approval. "Yours is a country with a great future, young lady. My name is Silas Shatner."

"I'm pleased to meet you." A little self-consciously Pamela put out her hand, which was clasped by the long, boney, brown-spotted appendage at the end of Shatner's skinny arm. "Bill Kent," said the large young man, smiling and holding out his hand also.

"I work at the Canadian embassy," said Pamela after a small pause.

"How do you like Washington?" The two men asked the question together and stopped, laughing. Pamela was grateful to be able to join in. "I love it," she replied. "There's so much richness and history. How about you? Do you live here?"

"No, we're from New England," said Kent. His smile kept sending small shock waves through Pamela's heart. "We're just visiting here."

Shatner looked at his watch, then slyly at Pamela. "We were planning a bite of lunch. Would you care to join us?" he asked.

Pamela hesitated only a moment. She nodded. "I'd love to," she said. They walked down a pathway lined with still-bare cherry trees. A gusty March wind blew in from the Potomac, and Pamela watched a solitary gull balancing effortlessly on the breeze. They ate at a small rathskeller where the sauerbraten was cooked and served by an old German who told them he had come to America with his parents in 1903.

Just before they got up to leave, Kent looked at Pamela with a puzzled smile on his face and said, "I feel like I've met you before—but I'm sure I haven't." Pamela just smiled. She really didn't know what to say. But she knew that she shared the same feeling. She also had a sensing that somehow or other she would be seeing Kent again.

Alone in her apartment later that evening, Pamela thought back to the events that had led her to visit the Lincoln Memorial. She had originally planned to go for a drive to Williamsburg with a friend from the Embassy. But the previous evening, Donald had phoned to say that he was sick and would not be able to make the trip. Pamela was disappointed, for she had heard much about the old colonial capital, and it left her with little time to make plans for the holiday. Next morning, she decided to visit the Lincoln shrine and the Tidal basin. It didn't seem an exciting way to fill the day but it was better than nothing, and with her friends all busy or away there weren't many options.

What a fragile chain of events, she reflected, led her to be at the Lincoln Memorial at the same time as William and the professor. Was it all coincidence? She wondered. But she did not spend too long pondering a question she could not answer. Bill Kent kept reappearing in her consciousness and she did not mind at all. What was it about him that intrigued her so? She was still puzzling about it when she drifted off to sleep.

Chapter IX

1953

It was a beautiful summer day in the City, that golden square mile of London where financial institutions jam tightly together in streets with names like Poultry, Threadneedle and Throgmorton. James Beresford, a director of Levy and Beresford, the merchant bankers, looked at his watch and stepped out to keep his luncheon engagement with Archie Mayfield, a stockbroker friend. Levy and Beresford was a long-established firm. It had been founded during the Napoleonic War, when a young immigrant called Jacob Levy took the profits from his sales of gentlemen's shoes and started a small merchant banking business in Cheapside.

"I hear you're off to Scotland tomorrow," said Beresford as he broke off a piece of French bread and put some Brie on it. "I need your advice, old boy. Some money has come my way and I want to put it into something."

"How much are you talking about?" Archie fished a piece of kidney out of his steak and kidney pudding. The hubbub of talking around them virtually drowned their conversation.

"Ten thousand pounds," said Beresford.

Archie Mayfield, a younger man by five or six years—he had been just too young for service in the war—chewed on his piece of kidney and looked thoughtfully into his tankard.

"Something that might interest you, James," he said, draining his glass, "is Armstrong Motors. Their five shilling shares are up to eight shillings, and likely to keep going up, as far as we can tell."

"Armstrong Motors? That's Lord Brooker's company, isn't it?"

"Right. He took it over two years ago. I think it's a good bet, actually."

"I like the sound of it. Would you go ahead, old chap?"

"Ten thousand? Righty-ho."

Their conversation drifted on. Mayfield asked after Julia, who had been sick with a nasty bout of flu for several days. They took a few minutes to analyze a classic innings by Dennis Compton and discuss a promising new racehorse. Mayfield purchased the shares for Beresford that afternoon, and the next day was on his way north for a climbing holiday. When the news of the proposed takeover of Armstrong Motors by a well-known consortium hit the City two days later—causing trading in Armstrong shares to be temporarily suspended on the Stock Exchange—Mayfield was halfway up the peak of Ben Nevis and knew nothing of the event. Rumours flew in all directions like startled pigeons, but one thing that was very clear was that Armstrong Motors shares would be going up substantially in value.

The Bank of England, the Old Lady of Threadneedle Street, stands at the centre of the "Square Mile." It is a massive, fortress-like building with high stone walls that are devoid of windows. From this focal point, the streets of Cornhill, Lombard, Poultry and Threadneedle radiate like spokes of a wheel, each lined with banks of various descriptions. The doors of the Bank of England are guarded by pink-coated footmen. Past one of these footmen, at 10:43 a.m., hurried recently knighted Sir Reginald Beresford, chairman of Levy and Beresford, on his way to meet with the Bank Governor.

"Reginald, my dear chap," the Governor exclaimed, shaking his hand warmly. "How good to see you. Do sit down."

The Governor seated himself behind his rather large, austere desk and gazed with penetrating blue eyes at his guest. "No point in beating about the bush," he said quietly. "It's about this Armstrong Motors business. I hear your boy bought into them rather heavily just before the takeover was announced. Pure coincidence, I'm sure, but I thought I should have a word with you."

"Of course."

"Have you had a chance to speak with him yet?"

"Not yet, I'm afraid. I only heard about it myself yesterday." Sir Reginald spoke casually, but the other man sensed the pain in his words. His face softened. They had been friends a long time.

"As I say, I'm sure there was nothing underhanded, Reginald, but it is rather a nuisance. You know how the gutter press love to get hold of these things. Ah well, as long as the boy learns a lesson from it all, eh?"

A butler came bearing a tray with tea. Sir Reginald helped himself to cream and sugar, stirring in more lumps than he usually allowed himself. There were a few more questions from the Governor, but soon their talk turned to more comfortable matters, including the Governor's recent move into farming at an estate in Suffolk. Sir Reginald took his leave at 11:20 and returned to his office.

Miss Jane Effingham had been personal secretary to Sir Reginald for fifteen years. It was not a job that anyone else in the bank would have fancied particularly, but she seemed to thrive on it. Her role was that of a peacemaker. She not only coped with the domineering behaviour that tended to find expression through the chairman, particularly in times of stress; she also presented a consistently friendly, reasonable face to the rest of the staff.

Perhaps, with her woman's intuition, Jane Effingham sensed the underlying factors that made Sir Reginald behave as he did. Certainly she was aware of the tremendous void which had been left in his life when his wife had died. She alone also knew the physical and mental pain which he had suffered since his experiences in the First World War. Even now, thirty-five years later, that suffering still showed in the eyes of Reginald Algernon Beresford, M.C., hero of Champigny Ridge.

His mood was a black one when he returned from his visit to the Governor of the Bank of England. Even the hall porter, one of the most stolid and imperceptive of men, was aware of it as he came into the building. Miss Effingham saw it immediately, and braced herself in the way a small boat sailor will secure his ship before a storm. Sir Reginald, passing through his outer office, did not even look at her. "Tell James I want to see him," he said sharply. The next instant he had passed through into his own office, shutting the door loudly behind him.

Miss Effingham decided to deliver the message personally. The news of the coming takeover of Armstrong Motors had appeared in all the newspapers the previous day. She was aware also, as most of the staff were, of rumours circulating in the City that James Beresford had bought heavily into Armstrong Motors a short while before the news of the takeover was released. It was not difficult to guess the reason for Sir Reginald's sudden visit to the Bank of England, or his abrupt request to see his only son. Like almost everyone else at Levy and Beresford, Miss Effingham was immensely fond of James. His warm smile and outgoing personality brought a refreshingly human touch into the business.

Jane handled her employer's message as if it were a land mine.

"I'm afraid he looks a bit grim, Mr. Beresford," she whispered with characteristically British understatement. "I'm sorry."

Why on earth should you apologize? thought James. But he did not say it. Instead he smiled as he looked up at her. "I like the new hairdo, Effie," he said. "I'm waiting for a call from New York. Tell him I'll be in to see him as soon as I've taken it, will you?"

Jane Effingham blushed slightly as she walked away. No one else called her "Effie"—or commented on her hairstyle.

James knocked on the door of the chairman's office and stepped inside. "You wanted to see me, Dad?" he said. The room was a period piece. Two or three portraits, one a drawing of the founder, hung on the richly panelled wall behind his father. An antique clock ticked away on the mantelpiece above the marble fireplace. The desk at which Sir Reginald sat was intricately carved and more than two hundred years old.

James could see it was going to be heavy. Oppression hung in the room like old cigar smoke. He knew well the false calm that preceded an attack of his father's temper.

"I want to talk to you about this Armstrong Motors business," said Sir Reginald. "I was just called over to see the Governor. He's not happy, not happy at all." Suddenly, his father's control slipped. Like a ship breaking away from its moorings in a storm, he lost his temper. "How in God's name could you do it?" he roared. "You obviously had inside information and used it to your own advantage. Did you stop to think of the effect this would have on the bank? Did you?"

"Dad, please . . ."

"I've only seen this happen once before in all the years I've been with Levy and Beresford. What do you think it will do to our clients' trust?" He glowered at his son, his face twitching.

"But I didn't have inside information." He was angry himself now. He couldn't help it. His father launched into another round of recrimination, but he cut in.

"I had no inside information," he said loudly, almost shouting.

As suddenly as it had begun, the storm peaked. The barometric needle hovered somewhere between "very low" and "low." His father's lips compressed into a tight line.

"You say you didn't have inside information?"

"That's right. None whatsoever. Archie Mayfield just said it was a good company and he thought their shares would go up."

His father sat back in his chair. He looked five or ten years older. He shook his head.

"My God," he said softly, almost as if to himself. "If only I could believe you."

The words cut James like a knife. They hurt worse than his father's diatribe. He stood up, his expression growing cold.

"That's something you'll have to make your own mind up about, sir," he said. He felt sick. His throat congested and he had to cough to clear it as he spoke. He knew he was reacting now, just as his father had done, but he did not care. He turned, made for the door.

"James . . ." his father started.

"I've got to go. There's nothing more to say." He grasped the doorknob, turned it and let himself out, ignoring the words his father was trying to say. He walked quickly by Miss Effingham, ignoring her too.

Jane Effingham watched Beresford disappear through the outer door of her office into the hallway with something akin to panic. The look on his face as he swung past her with barely a glance in her direction frightened her. She had heard—couldn't help it—some of the conversation that had passed between him and his father. Clearly, the situation was serious. She felt an urge to do something. What could she do, though? She shook her head impatiently, picked up her purse, and hurried out of her office. "Please tell Sir Reginald that I'll be out for a few minutes," she told the switchboard lady as she passed by.

Outside, she saw Beresford crossing the street. She caught up with him. "Please, Mr. Beresford, may I talk to you?" she asked beseechingly. He turned, a look of anger and annoyance in his eyes.

"I think I'd rather be alone," he said. "If you don't mind." She tried to be calm. She knew she couldn't give up.

"Please, just a few minutes?" she pleaded. "I know I shouldn't be interfering but I feel somebody's got to try to help."

People hurried by, mostly men in formal dark suits, some wearing top hats. He looked at her, his mouth grim, his lips tightened and turned down at the corners. His face relaxed a little. "Oh what the hell. Let's have a drink," he said. "But I won't be very good company."

"Mr. Beresford," she said, when they were seated at a table. "I haven't known your father as long as you, of course, but I've known him a long time. I know how difficult he can be, how unreasonable. But he doesn't mean it. He really doesn't. It's just that he's been badly hurt in his life and he hasn't been able to come to terms with it all."

"A lot of us have been badly hurt. It doesn't give us an excuse to climb all over people. In any case it's not the point." His eyes were cold again. "He doesn't trust me, Effie."

"Oh but I think you're wrong," she cried. "He does really. He was just confused and upset."

"He was that all right."

"He was upset by all the nasty rumours going around. And don't forget he'd just been called in to see the Governor."

Beresford took a pull at his beer. She was old enough to be his mother, he thought.

"I'm going to resign." The words came out bitterly, without premeditation, almost without thought.

"James . . ." It was the first time she had addressed him by his first name. She stopped, embarrassed.

"If we can't trust one another what have we got, Effie? Skiffington can have my job, the sycophantic bastard, he wants it badly enough."

"Over my dead body." Jane Effingham looked like a mother lion that had lost its cubs. My God, Beresford thought, despite her good nature I wouldn't want to get on the wrong side of her. "I mean it, Mr. Beresford. I really don't think the bank would survive if you left. You may not realize it—perhaps you don't want to right now—but we need you. So does your father. Don't do anything hasty, please. Your father is a very proud man. If you take too many steps away from each other you may never find one another again." Her voice faltered. She took a hanky out of her purse and wiped her eyes.

"I'm sorry," she sniffed. "I'm becoming emotional."

"You really mean what you're saying, don't you?"

"Of course I mean it!" she said, with a touch of defiance.

A barmaid came over, attractive in a plump kind of way, and cleared some glasses from the table. She smiled at Beresford, who was too preoccupied to notice.

"It must be difficult being so good-looking," Jane Effingham said, looking at him naughtily. He felt the tension ease out of him. He knew one thing. If he was going to make peace with his father he must do it straight away, just as he had insisted on going back into action straight away the first time he was shot down. That was a lesson his father had taught him. He had bought him a horse on his tenth birthday, and he got thrown off when it suddenly took off. His dad had caught up with the creature and spoken to it. He had been impressed with how gently he spoke and how delicately he handled the animal. Much more delicately than he usually handled people. His father had insisted that he climb back on the horse immediately.

Yes. If something was to be resolved between them it must be resolved now, or it would be too late; he felt it intuitively and he knew that he had already made a decision. Difficult and overbearing though the old boy might be at times, it wasn't right the way he had stormed out of the room in a huff, paying no attention when he tried to call him back. It had been a reaction, pure and simple; a desire to hurt back. Now, a quiet voice told him he and his father should at least talk about it some more.

He smiled, a light back in his eyes. "Thanks for coming after me, Effie," he said. They made their way back to the bank.

His father was still sitting at his desk. He looked up, surprised, as he knocked and walked in. James saw a look of relief pass over his father's face, replaced the next moment by his habitual rather stern expression.

"Yes?" said his father.

"I'm sorry I hurried out," he said. He walked up to the desk and sat down. Looking at his father's lined, worried face, he felt a sudden compassion for him. "If you would like me to resign, sir, I'll be glad to do so," he said quietly. "But I had no inside information about Armstrong Motors."

His father cleared his throat.

"I believe you," he said. "Of course I believe you." He peered at James over the top of his spectacles. "And what nonsense is this about resigning? As a matter of fact, James . . ." His dad paused, and cleared his throat again. "There's something I want to tell you. I'm planning to retire next year. I need a rest. I'd like you to take over. As you know, there has always been a Levy or a Beresford in the position of senior partner or chairman. The line of Jacob Levy has finished, so a great deal depends upon you, James. Will you take the job?"

He had expected his father to remain in the saddle for at least two or three more years. His request came as an utter surprise. But as he looked over his father's shoulder at the portrait of Jacob Levy, James Beresford felt no hesitation. It wasn't just a matter of duty or obligation. It was the challenge and adventure which the opportunity offered.

"I will," he said. He added softly, "I feel honoured, sir. Thank you."

"Capital. Capital. Let's have a drink." His father beamed and went to a cupboard. He mixed two drinks, handing one to his son. "You don't know how glad this makes me, my boy."

"Dad?"

"Yes?"

"Could we invite Miss Effingham to join us?"

Two days later Archie Mayfield returned from his holiday in Scotland and came to see James and his father.

"God, I feel terrible about all this," he said, as he took a seat in the chairman's office. "I read about it in the papers yesterday as I was travelling down. I had no idea. It's all nonsense of course. I'm making a statement to the Governor and the newspapers this afternoon. James had no inside information, and neither did I. My recommendation was based on a report which a chap in my firm boned up for me—young Peabody. Here, I thought you might like to see a copy of it. Keep it if you like. God, what a mess." Archie Mayfield took out a large white handkerchief and wiped his brow.

* * *

William Tolliver Kent III always enjoyed the drive to his mother's estate, Southwind, in northwest Connecticut. As he headed west out of Hartford, he thought of the many times his mother had refused to leave her beloved ancient home and move closer to the younger folks. He didn't blame her, really, for he had inherited a good dose of independence himself.

He knew that the vigorous matriarch's second question—after a discreet inquiry about his love life—would be about the activities of Kent Industries, of which he was managing director. Following his father's death his mother had become the major stockholder in the family company.

This time he made the journey with his younger brother Jed, second-in-command since William took over running of the business.

"There's something I want to share with you, Jed," said Kent quietly as the city of Hartford disappeared behind them. Jed looked at him questioningly. "I've had an offer to go into politics."

"Politics?" His brother frowned.

"Congressman Davidson asked to see me on my last trip to Washington. He's retiring at the end of his term because of his health, though it's not common knowledge. He wants to back someone he likes, and asked if I would be willing to be a candidate."

"It's a tough business." Jed was still frowning.

"That's for sure. Davidson is worried about where the country is going."

"I don't blame him."

"He thinks McCarthy will split the nation in two if we're not careful. I agree with him."

Jed nodded. "I remember John Davidson patting me on the head when I was about twelve," he said. He paused. "Someone said he is one of half a dozen honest men in the House."

"I think there are more than that."

"Don't count on it, big brother. But what about the business? Would you have to quit?"

Kent rubbed his chin reflectively. "I don't know. I'd have to see. Of course there's no guarantee I'd get the nomination anyway. John just said he had spoken with a few people and they liked the idea."

"He's a powerful man. His support would mean a lot. But suppose you got yourself nominated and won the primary . . . Are you sure you want to get into that rat race, Bill? Look at the way people like McCarthy and McCarran are tearing the hides off innocent people. Look at the way the oilmen buy up support and screw anyone who gets in the way." Jed was getting into his stride.

William broke in. "All the more reason someone has to stand up and be counted," he said.

Jed looked at him intently. "You really have a feeling about this, don't you? Like when you joined the OSS?"

The older Kent smiled, charm flowing naturally through him like the force of wind or sun. "Maybe I do," he said.

"We're different, you know," said Jed, now serious and analytical. "I don't mind being comfortable. In fact, I like it. But you don't. Although you're easygoing on the surface, underneath you're an adventurer. A hundred years ago you'd have been heading your wagon west to Oregon. Anyway"—he caught his brother's eye and winked—"I'm with you, whatever the hell you do."

"Thanks, Jed." He thumped the younger man's shoulder. Jed winced.

They drove past a field brilliant with the large, glossy leaves and yellow-green blossoms of laurels.

"There's something else."

Jed looked at him, a whimsical glint in his eye. "Yeah? You're getting married?"

"Let's say Pam and I are getting serious. I want to bring her out to meet Mom on my next trip."

"Now that's something to celebrate. In fact, it's the best news I've heard in years." He and his brother laughed aloud.

"Boy, will Mother ever be glad to hear that. It'll make her day," Jed continued enthusiastically. "I've only met her once or twice but Pamela sure has my vote. No wonder you've been making so many trips to Washington." He paused. "If you want a best man, feel free to ask," he said.

They drove through Canton and Winsted, preparing for its Laurel Festival, and on toward Canaan. Presently they branched off and finally came to a stop in front of an elegant Colonial-style mansion with a freshly painted exterior. A short, immensely dignified man came out to meet them, limping slightly on one leg. Arnold Piggee had been wounded in France in the First World War. His face was creased in an enormous welcoming grin that showed teeth still dazzlingly white in spite of his advancing years.

"Welcome, Master William and Master Jed," he said, nodding at each in turn. He picked up their suitcases. "Mrs. Kent will be very pleased to see you. She is waiting in the lounge."

"Samantha busy in the kitchen, Arnold?"

The black man laughed heartily. "Very busy. She is making a game pie, I believe."

Jed excused himself and went upstairs. "Tell Mother I'll see her in a few minutes," he called.

Rose Esmeralda Kent was the widow of Arthur J. Kent, a well-known New England industrialist who started out as a silverware manufacturer but later built up a thriving tool-making business. Kent Industries now exported to more than thirty countries.

"How wonderful to see you again, William," said Mrs. Kent, looking affectionately at her older son. The two were alone in what had once been her husband's study, but was now her office. Afternoon sunlight streamed through the recently installed picture window. Although she was in her seventies, Mrs. Kent looked a trim sixty if that. A few acquaintances said it must be because she spent a lot of money on her cosmetician. As far as William Kent was concerned it was because his mother, who had been one of five daughters of an immigrant Rumanian prince, had found the Grail of peace. It hadn't always been so. As a boy and into his teens he could remember some fierce arguments between his mother and his father, arguments that would end in shouting and red-rimmed eyes, his own at times. But at some point, perhaps in handling the death of her husband, and later his own absence in what was often dirty and dangerous work in the war, she had come to a point of resolution in herself which no longer fought against circumstances but accepted them and blessed them for what they were. "To think, William, that I was 65 before I realized you can give thanks in any situation," she had said as they walked through the grounds of Southwind after his return from Europe in 1945.

As he faced his mother now and told her what was on his mind, he knew that he would not meet with resistance. There would be no endeavour to manipulate him. But her wisdom and intuition were very important to him.

"Do you think it's foolish, Mother?" he asked. "I've heard it said that politicians are either fools or dishonest—fools if they think they can change anything, dishonest if they are trying to feather their own nests. But John Davidson touched something in me. He's not a fool and I know he's not dishonest. He's just terribly concerned about what is happening to the country."

His mother smiled. "Someone has to be a politician," she said, "obviously. Personally I don't see why a politician can't be honest. Oh, I suppose they have to do some compromising to be effective, but . . ." her forehead puckered in thought, "as long as there is a certain point beyond which you won't go. That's really the point, I think." Mrs. Kent looked at her son with keen, appraising eyes. "There is no question about that in your case," she continued, with a certain pride. "If you feel you have something to offer, you should offer it, just like John Davidson or your friend Jack Kennedy. Abraham Lincoln was a politician and he certainly wasn't a fool or dishonest. Here. Give your mother a hug."

Chapter X

1953

The special announcement from Radio Moscow was accompanied by an appeal from the Central Committee and the Council of Ministers for the Soviet people to redouble their "unity, solidarity, fortitude of spirit and vigilance in these troubled days." As the broadcast came to a close the middle-aged woman with the fine, tired eyes and thick black hair switched off the radio and stared at the picture on the wall near her desk. The picture showed two young soldiers posing in a small garden with roses blooming behind them. They were laughing at the camera, arms around each other's shoulders, obviously proud in their new army uniforms. The woman rose and took the photograph down from the wall and held it tightly. Tears fell. However, they were tears of relief, for the little seed of hope that she had nurtured for so long and which seemed to have died was alive again. It sprouted shoots even as she sat there, holding the picture, swaying gently in the chair, remembering.

How ready and eager they had both been to fight, her sons, Leonid, the elder, and Grigori, when they had heard the news of the German onslaught. And how quickly they had vanished into the maw of the Red Army, giving her just a quick hug and kiss and then climbing excitedly into the train that was waiting to take them away. Six months later Leonid was gravely wounded near Rostov and died without regaining consciousness. Grigori always had a natural bent for writing—his essays had won several prizes at school—but with the rigors of war his letters had been few. How she treasured them when they arrived, sometimes after a long and incredibly difficult journey. She would open the battered envelopes with trembling fingers and savour their contents for months.

Then, just when it seemed as if the war was coming to a close and she would be seeing her son again, the news came that he had been sent to a prison camp in Siberia. She had pleaded for information from army and NKVD authorities, but all she had ever been able to find out was that her son had been sentenced to ten years hard labour for aiding a counterrevolutionary by the name of Sergeant Mihailovich. Numbed by her inability to penetrate the wall of red tape and bureaucracy and disturbed by a suggestion from a sour-faced NKVD colonel that it would be in her own best interests to stop making a fuss—she might, he implied, end up being routed to Siberia herself—she had finally accepted the inevitable. But she prayed for her son twice a day every day, though she had never thought of herself as a religious person.

There was a loud knocking at her door and she heard excited voices outside. "Come in, come in," she called, hurrying to the door. There stood Yevgeni, the retired postman, and Natalia, her next-door neighbour, a thin, unhappy woman whose husband was a sailor. Natalia's man was not often home but when he was he spent his time sleeping with her, shouting at her and drinking. The whole apartment block heaved a sigh of relief when her husband's leave came to a close and he had to pack up his bag and hurry away. And behind Natalia stood Maria, large, placid, cheerful, who had never been known to lose her temper. Maria came from Yakutsk, where her husband had been a ship's captain on the Lena River.

They came bursting in through the doorway chattering like a flock of blackbirds. Even Maria was excited, her ample bosom heaving as she spoke. "Alla, did you hear the news?" she called out. "Stalin is ill. It just came over the radio."

"A cerebral hemorrhage, they say. He was in his Moscow apartment," Yevgeni chimed in.

"The Patriarch and the Chief Rabbi have ordered special services to be held. It must be very serious," said Natalia.

Alla Antonieva faced them with a calm smile. "Yes, I heard the news," she said. "Come, let's have a cup of tea."

They sat and discussed the situation, sipping the strong black tea from hand-painted china cups. "He'll be dead in a day or two, you'll see," Yevgeni asserted. "They would never make an announcement like this if he had any sort of chance."

"It's the end," Natalia kept saying. "It's the end. Who else can keep the country together? They'll be fighting each other like hyenas."

There was a momentary quiet.

"Oh, Alla," said Maria suddenly, very excited. "Perhaps it will mean changes. They may release Grigori."

They all looked at Alla, who smiled. "Yes," she said. "It is possible. I pray that it will be so." Her voice broke and she could not speak anymore. Yevgeni put a gentle hand on her shoulder.

"I agree with Maria," he said. "There will be changes, you'll see. It would not surprise me at all if Grigori comes home."

Her hand reached out and held his for a moment. The tears had dried now. "Thank you, Yevgeni," she said.

It was unreal. He had been nine years in this place. Nine years holding the hands of dying men and listening to Arkady, the thin, intense young dissident with advanced pneumonia, parading around the floor in his ragged underwear as he recited his latest poems of love, hope and faith. Nine years labouring in cold and heat, living on scraps of bread and soup, and learning that the key to survival was spiritual stamina and not physical stamina. Now the whole scene was dissolving before his eyes.

Parasha, the prison telegraph, had brought news that following Stalin's death a commission from Moscow was making the rounds of the camps and ordering wholesale releases. Hundreds of thousands of prisoners were being classified as "totally rehabilitated," pardoned, and sent by train to Moscow. The commission was expected to arrive at Ust-Ulenov at any time. Guards who had been coarse and unfeeling suddenly began trying to behave like human beings. Kosigin, one of the worst, actually smiled at Grigori one morning. The commandant himself, Colonel Borokov, shook his hand and asked after his health. The prison status of the barracks was lifted, and the locks taken off the doors, although the perimeter wall was still guarded by machine guns. On one memorable morning the prisoners ripped their number patches off their caps and clothes. No official order to that effect had been received in the camp, but the prison telegraph heard that it was expected. The prisoners simply anticipated the order. Camp authorities made no attempt at reprisals, nor did they threaten the inmates.

Grigori Antoniev's release took exactly one minute and three seconds on a pleasant Thursday afternoon two weeks after the commission arrived and began their work. He had spotted his name on the list posted outside the administration building. There was no difficulty in spotting it. It fairly leaped out at him! He waited impatiently with a group of other prisoners for his turn. A man would climb some steps and enter the room where the commission was sitting. The door would close. Within a minute, as a rule, although sometimes it took longer, the door would open and the man would reemerge. In some instances, a release was deferred; there were special circumstances to be taken into account and a man might be told his case would come up again in a few months. But for most, the appearance before the commission was a mere formality.

A man would often come back outside jumping up and down like a five-year-old, or so affected emotionally that he stumbled like an alcoholic. Some sat down on the ground as if in a trance. A few just packed up their things, shook hands with their friends and said "Good-bye" as if they merely had been spending a few days at a holiday resort. The KGB colonel who was heading up the four-man commission looked at Grigori with tired, red eyes and asked the prosecutor's representative if there were any special circumstances. Grigori held his breath. The man merely shook his head. And what was the colonel thinking about? Did he wonder about how they had suffered? Did he wonder why men who for the most part had committed no crime rightfully punishable by a prison sentence of any kind, let alone a slave labour camp, had been incarcerated in such places for ten or twenty years? The official made a small gesture with his right hand. "You are free to go, Antoniev," he said in a voice so weary that Grigori had to strain to hear. "You have been fully pardoned."

He left the camp with a large group of other ex-prisoners three days later, after transportation arrangements had been worked out and documents issued. All his belongings were packed in a worn kit-bag which he had neatly repaired in two or three places. He wondered if anyone would ever believe him if he said that, while he had endured much misery at Ust-Ulenov, he had also experienced tremendous happiness and peace. It was as if he had penetrated to the core of life. Sometimes, sharing some mouldy bread with another prisoner, he had felt closer to a fellow human being than he would ever have thought possible.

Well, it would all be in his book, the book which for safety's sake he had kept in his head, although in recent weeks, with the relaxed conditions in the camp, he had begun quietly making a few notes on paper. As he looked down at his kit-bag he could not help chuckling to himself. Anyone who rummaged through that kit-bag would think he had little with him, but he carried something extra which was not presently visible—the beginnings of a book which he knew would shake the world. He could still hear the faint voice of the poet Arkady, battling its way through the sludge in his lungs a few minutes before he died, saying, "You mean it, Grigori? You're putting me in your book?" Yes, Arkady was in the book, and his friend Andropovich, who had helped him survive, and had been amongst the first to be released, and Zavrenov, the mad-dog guard, and Kuznetkin, the gang leader, and Gorelov, the Latvian, and above all, the sergeant, his beloved sergeant, who had died a hero's death—not, ironically, fighting the Germans, but his own countrymen.

Grigori Antoniev's truck rolled through the open gates of the camp and gathered speed along the road to the station.

* * *

Congressman Lennard was pleased with himself. The last witness, a fat smoothie from the State Department, was a pile of jelly by the time they finished with him. The proceedings were being televised. The current hearings were bringing his name into prominence far beyond the confines of Washington. And in many ways the whole thing was duck soup! Not many people called before the committee dared offer resistance anymore. They had learned that to defy was to risk a jail sentence. Under the bright kleig lights Lennard stroked the lobe of his right ear with his forefinger and prepared to strike a further blow to keep America safe from Communism.

"Your name, please?" he asked, his attention on the papers in front of him. It was a ploy of which he was rather fond. At a suitable moment, he would look up, thrust his craggy head forward, and project the full force of his position and power at the unfortunate individual sitting in front of him.

"Silas Shatner."

"Ah yes. Mr. Shatner. You're a professor at McGibbon College, I believe?"

"I am."

Something in the timbre of the voice rang a little alarm in Congressman Lennard's sensitive antennae. He looked up sharply, sooner than he had intended to. Yes, Professor Shatner did not look like a pushover. He must tread carefully.

He sat back in his chair, drawing strength from his fellow committee members and from the solid antiquity of the oak-panelled hearing room.

"Professor Shatner," he said weightily. "Are you now or have you ever been a Communist?"

The answer was direct and unequivocal. "At one point in my life, yes. I joined the Communist Party and was a member for a few months in 1931."

"I see." It was going to be easier than he thought. Congressman Lennard toyed some more with his ear-lobe. Congressman Jameson, an ambitious young man who had been appointed to the committee only two weeks previously, cut in. "And why did you become a Communist?"

"Young man, I didn't like what was happening in the country. Things were going to hell in a handcart and the established parties seemed about as effective as two possums in a paper bag. I wanted to see if there was a better way."

"And what did you decide?"

"I decided that Communism was even more ineffective and futile."

Congressman Jameson hesitated for a moment, decided to stand his ground. He said coldly, "Are you saying you've had no further association with the Commies since that time?"

"I am indeed. I sent them a letter that told them what I thought of them in very plain language. Want to see a copy of the letter?"

Congressman Lennard decided to regain the initiative. "Perhaps you could help us, Professor Shatner," he said, leaning forward and smiling like a friendly barracuda. "My colleagues and I would like to know who your acquaintances were during that time when, as you admit, you were a Communist. Give us some names, Professor. We'd be real obliged and America would thank you too."

Professor Shatner smiled back, though his eyes were as hard as pieces of grey granite.

"I'd like to help you, Mr. Chairman, I really would. I appreciate what you folks are doing here, protecting the American soul and the American way of life. I love that soul and that way of life as much as any of you do. But I can't answer that question."

"Are you invoking the Fifth Amendment, Professor?"

"I am."

"Don't want to help us on that, eh?" Congressman Lennard scratched his ear-lobe and looked thoughtful. He could feel his ulcer acting up a bit. He'd decided they weren't going to get too far with this tough-minded old coot. Hell, he wasn't much of a catch anyway. He didn't know why his staffers had suggested bringing him up.

"Let me ask you another question." It was the cool, incisive Congressman from Illinois. "What can you tell us about the activities of the Communist Party during the time you were involved with them?"

Professor Shatner shook his head. "Not too much, I'm afraid." He looked genuinely regretful. "I was only at a few meetings. It sounded all very half-baked to me, and like I say, I just quit."

"You're not being very helpful," said Congressman Jameson. "Sure you won't change your mind and give us some names?"

Silas Shatner sat dignified and immovable. "I'm sorry," he said.

Chairman Lennard put a hand to his stomach, hoping to quiet his ulcer.

They tossed a few more questions around, for form's sake as much as anything, and then they let him go. The next witness that morning promised to be a whole lot more interesting. She was a former Hollywood movie star now living in New York. The word from their staffers was that she had some sensational stuff to unload that would rate front-page coverage. Shatner pulled himself to his full, and considerable, height, stared frostily at the men sitting at the long table, and took his leave. The damage had already been done, of course. When he returned to New Hampshire and his college he was called in for an important meeting by the president and two trustees. Although he had tenure, he was dismissed. "Intellectual arrogance before a Congressional committee," they said, when he asked upon what grounds.

Teaching was Shatner's life. It was highly unlikely that he would be able to find another post. But apart from getting uncommonly angry, he made no effort to beg or beseech. The dean and trustees felt as uncomfortable as hell, of course, but what can you do? each said to himself. One recalled a Biblical quote to the effect it was better that one man should lose his life than that the whole nation should perish.

"How do you guys feel about Joe McCarthy?" the ironworker near the rear of the hall shouted. Kent felt a stir of interest. The last exchange on milk prices had not exactly had the audience on the edge of their seats. The moderator turned to each of the two candidates, smiling. "Who would like to go first?" he asked.

But Congressman Harrison Waite, 60, was already off and running. It was the moment he had been waiting for. The advice of his campaign man all along had been to portray himself as an enemy of Communism, while at the same time questioning Kent's approach in this regard. "Make it seem he's soft on Commies and you've got him," he had said. "It worked well for Nixon, didn't it?" Yes, he was a shrewd one all right, his manager. Harrison Waite opened his mouth and put it into top gear.

"I'm very glad this has come up because it's a very important question," he said, running his quick brown eyes over the crowd. "I dare say Senator Joseph McCarthy sometimes makes mistakes, but believe me, ladies and gentlemen, the evil which he is fighting, which he is giving his life to fight, is a very real evil. It's a threat to our whole way of life. It's a threat to our children, our institutions, everything we stand for. The Russians aren't ordinary, civilized people. They plan to take over the world and impose their godless society on God-fearing people. By the way, don't forget they've got the atom bomb now! You ask what I feel about Joe McCarthy, friend? He's doing a damn sight more good than bad. And let me add this. It's my belief that every true American who loves his country has a duty to fight Communism wherever and whenever it shows its evil, treacherous face."

He paused, then lowered his voice dramatically. "Ladies and gentlemen, I think you know that in my four years as Congressman representing this great region of our country, I've shown where my love lies . . . for this great land we call America! Whatever it takes to resist the Red menace, count on me to do it. God bless you, ladies and gentlemen, and I ask for your support again for a second term. Thank you."

Harrison Waite sat back, well pleased with himself. He had, he felt, projected sincerity, spontaneity, and concern. His seasoned political antennae told him he had moved his audience. That was it! Raise the spectre of Russia and you got 'em moved. And dammit wasn't it the truth? Wasn't it the truth those damned Russians wanted to take over the world? Harrison caught the happy expression on his campaign man's face and grinned at him. The hall became silent. The moderator looked at Kent. In the middle of the fourth row Kent saw Pamela looking serious.

"Senator McCarthy may mean well," said Kent, speaking slowly and deliberately, "but in my view what is happening under the name of McCarthyism is stirring up fear and hatred in this country that could tear us apart." He paused, checking his audience. With one or two exceptions they seemed cold. Some were fidgetting. His campaign advisor had not wanted him to come to this meeting, warning that the sponsoring organization favoured Waite. Kent had taken the attitude that as a newcomer on the scene, and in some respects the underdog, he had to take risks. And so here he was. He was going to speak the truth as he saw it.

"It's all going too far," he went on, speaking more quickly, hoping to change the mood. "Innocent men and women are being victimized and ruined. Take the Rader case. Here's a man who was accused by government witnesses of having enrolled in a Communist Party summer school in New York in 1939 or '40. Yet he was able to prove he had never been east of the Rockies before 1945. Recently an actor in Hollywood committed suicide because he couldn't clear his name of the Communist stigma. This man was destroyed without ever having done anything harmful, let alone illegal, and this kind of thing is going on all the time in all parts of the country. Sure, we must be alert to the menace of Communism, but a witch hunt could lead us into the very state we're trying to avoid."

A few half-hearted rounds of applause greeted his words, but the boos were louder. Waite looked smug. A Waite supporter rose, an angry expression on her face. "May I ask Mr. Kent," she said, "if it is true that earlier this year he wrote a letter to the newspapers trying to defend a man who admitted to a Congressional committee that he had been a Communist?"

Kent nodded. "It's true," he said. He felt his big hands clenching and deliberately unclenched them. There must be a way through this impasse, he thought, but for the moment it escaped him. He kept on speaking even though he had no clear idea how to proceed.

"This man was, and is, a personal friend, a man of honour and integrity," he said. "He fought for this country in two wars. It's true he belonged to the Communist Party in 1931, but only for a few months, and when he saw their real intentions he left them permanently." He paused, feeling his way like a ship in a fog. He caught Pam's eye. "Go for broke," she seemed to be saying. Smoke from a cigar in the front row wafted up to his nostrils. His throat felt dry and he took a drink of water. Waite, the seasoned infighter, took advantage of the momentary pause and butted in.

His loud, demagogic voice penetrated to all corners of the hall, stirring emotions the way a chef stirs porridge. He vigorously waved a document, McCarthy style, as he spoke.

"I have in my hand," he shouted, "a revised version of a document that was compiled for the Dies Committee. This document lists the names of 35,000 Communists in the United States. Thirty-five thousand names, my friends. How many more are there that we don't know about? I remind you of the words of the anti-Communist patriot Herbert Philbrick. Where Communism is concerned, there is no one who can be trusted. Anyone can be a Communist—close friend, brother, employee or even employer, leading citizen, trusted public servant. As I say"—Waite liked to cover his flanks—"I'm not always happy with Senator McCarthy's approach, but if we're going to meet this menace in our midst it takes some guts." He clenched his free hand in a fist as he spoke and waved that too. "Just like Joe McCarthy," he added.

The audience was clearly with Waite. He looked around triumphantly. "I wonder if our young friend here has that kind of guts?" he asked, lowering his voice for effect. "Or being from a rich, well-to-do family as he is, maybe he's never seen hard times—doesn't know what it means to have to fight for something you believe in." There was a roar of applause from Waite supporters massed in the audience. His red, pudgy face gleamed as he sat down. He had not intended saying what he did at the end just yet. He had been carried away on the tide of emotion which he could feel being generated in the room, and had unleashed his personal attack in the heat of the moment. But it looked like it had got results.

Pamela stood up, her face flushed, defiance in her eyes. She had draped her coat around the chair behind her, and her red, woollen sweater accentuated her lovely figure. "Mr. Chairman, may I say a word, please?" she asked loudly. The room was suddenly quiet. Heads turned in her direction. Pamela quickly made her way to the front of the hall and stood facing the audience.

"I happen to know that what Mr. Waite just said is a lie," she declared. Despite the emotion in her voice, she was speaking clearly. In the momentary silence of the room her words went home with a quiet whoosh like arrows from a Comanche warrior's bow. "Mr. Kent—my husband—was studying at university in

1941 when he realized that while he and others sat comfortably in North America people across the ocean were fighting for their lives in the face of aggression and tyranny. He didn't have to get involved, but he did. He volunteered for the OSS, and was dropped behind enemy lines more than a dozen times. He fought with the partisans in Italy and Greece, and came close to death on many occasions. That's the man Mr. Waite was just talking about. Who would dare to say William Kent is not a patriot?" The room was now very quiet. Pamela looked for a moment at the faces in front of her. She turned, looked at the three men who sat on the stage, then smiled briefly at Kent. She walked back to her seat.

It was his chance. Kent stepped to the front of the stage, feeling his adrenalin pumping. He looked at the woman who had asked him about Shatner, and saw that her expression had changed. She was expectant now, rather than angry, looking at him closely.

"Without trust and tolerance I don't think America amounts to very much," he said. His normally easy-going voice was crackling with emotion. "It's part of the foundation of this country. McCarthyism in my view is hurting that foundation—making us more like the Soviets every day. Do we really want that?" He paused, letting his words drill home.

"He's right," an old lady with newly permed hair muttered to her neighbour. "He's right, you know."

"In Russia if you have strong political thoughts," Kent went on, "they send you off to a slave labour camp. Well, here you get locked in the pen for a year like Dashiell Hammett, or lose your job. What's the difference? A playwright who wants to say something different in Russia has to set his work in the seventeenth century. But it's the same here. The only play in North America that dares to speak out against McCarthyism is *The Crucible* by Arthur Miller, and guess what? It takes place in the seventeenth century too. Hell, we've had the Cincinnati Reds change their name to the Redlegs. The Harvard Russian Club became the Slavic Society. Thirty-four states have made it a felony to display a red flag." Kent paused, put his hand on his hip. He looked massive, immovable. "You know what it all adds up to?" he asked quietly. "A climate of fear and intolerance and conformity that is besmirching this country. I ask you, is that what made

America great? America got where it is because it had the courage to welcome new people and ideas, to explore new lands, to innovate and trust and dare. Those are my thoughts on McCarthyism. Thank you."

He sat down. The elderly lady in the third row clapped wildly, joined by many others. He was glad. But he knew he would have said what he said even if the audience had turned and ridiculed him. Afterwards, he was slightly annoyed with Pamela for having stuck her neck out in the meeting, and told her so. "Just leave the infighting to me, okay?" he said, squeezing her.

But Pamela was unrepentant. She smiled. "It worked, anyway, didn't it?" she said to him.

Chapter XI

1954

It was eleven in the evening and still Grigori pecked away at the ancient typewriter. Though he had already developed much of the book in his imagination in the camp, it took work to get it down on paper. Often he found himself staring at a blank piece of paper in the machine for fifteen or twenty minutes or longer, turning over possibilities, trying to decide how to develop a certain scene or chapter. It was solitary work, too. Just him and his typewriter and the four walls of the spare room in his mother's apartment. But he wasn't lonely, really, because constantly with him were the people in his book.

There was a knock on the door of the room. His mother called out. "Grigori? Can I come in?"

"Yes. Come in."

She had brought him a cup of tea. That was the ostensible reason for her visit, anyway. He could tell that she had something more on her mind. He sipped the tea thankfully.

She sat down on the empty chair beside the desk. Yes, he thought, she did have something on her mind. He folded his arms on top of the typewriter and looked at her, a smile on his bearded face. Lately, she was glad to see, his face had been filling out a bit, losing some of its gauntness.

"Grigori, I was talking with Anatalia Simonovna and she is angry that you have not yet been to visit them. She wants you to go there this weekend. Their daughter Tonya will be home. You know, the girl you used to try to kiss behind the woodshed? Of course, she was just a cheeky freckle-faced kid then, but you should see her now. My, how beautiful she is! Anyway, Anatalia said, 'Ask that son of yours please to come and visit us this weekend. We will have a special dinner and lots to drink, and there will be many nice people. We want to see him, Alla.' So of course I said I would speak to you. What do you think, Grigori? Can I tell her you will come?"

Grigori pursed his lips. She saw his smile fade. A little impatience crept into her voice. "Grigori, you cannot work all the time, it is not good for you. All day at the warehouse, and then all night at your desk, it is not natural. You need to get out and have some fun—meet some people your own age."

He looked at her with a hard, remote look, the one that had not been there before he went to the war. His voice was hard too, when he spoke. "Please thank Anatalia for the invitation, but I cannot go. I have to finish my book."

She felt her impatience increase and tried to push it down. "I know you have to finish but surely a little variety will be good for you. It will even help your book. I worry about you. You have missed so much . . . Don't you want to spend some time with a woman?"

Grigori sighed, nodded his head. "Yes, that would be very nice," he said. "Stop worrying, Mother. Later I will find a woman. But now I must finish what I have begun."

He saw that she was not entirely convinced, that she was searching for another argument. He bore down on her more roughly because he knew that she did not understand.

"It is because of all my friends who did not come back from the camps," he said. "I feel responsible to them. It is for their sake that I must work like this. Please. Leave me alone now."

Despite her worry, Alla Antonieva felt a sudden compassion for this man whom she had brought into the world and who had missed so many of the things that most young men experience. But at the same time she was touched by his strength and tenacity of character. There was a greatness in him which she could not deny. It would come out, she thought, and contribute something meaningful to the world.

Compulsively she touched him on his cheek. "I understand," she said. He took her hand for a moment, squeezed it. She rose silently and left the room. Down the hallway he heard a brief snatch of conversation. Yevgeni was pulling someone's leg, laughing in the way that always reminded Grigori of an inebriated duck. Grigori returned to his typewriter, his brow furrowed with concentration. People, scenes, times of terror and happiness crowded back into his memory. He saw his sergeant playing with the old man's dog in the farmhouse near the Desna. Saw his sergeant walking up to the guards in a final grand gesture of defiance . . . and dying, he did not doubt, at peace.

He began to type again. Only another hundred pages or so of *Sergeant Mihailovich* to write. He looked at his hands for a moment. Not the hands that one might associate with a writer, he thought. Muscular, worn, scarred, rough. But keep dancing along, fingers, keep pumping, blood and heart, keep functioning, nerves, lungs, stomach, we have a job to do together.

* * *

"He said I've got a retroverted uterus or something. I may never be able to have a baby."

Pamela Kent blurted the words out as she stood looking out of their living room window at the large elm tree which grew by the front gate. Then she began to cry, huge sobs that shook her whole body. She turned her face away as he went over to her.

"William, I feel terrible. What sort of life will we have without children? I can't bear to think that I won't be able to give you a child." The words came out in a torrent of self-reproach and bitterness. He put his arms around her, not saying a word. The powerful muscles tightened against her flesh and held her, gently but firmly. She pressed her face against his chest. He let her cry.

Gradually the sobs diminished. She turned her face slightly so that she could breathe more easily.

"I never dreamed I wouldn't be able to have a child," she said quietly. "This was something that happened to other women." She looked up at him. "I always thought I was normal."

"You are normal. And it's not that big a deal, Pam." His eyes met hers and conveyed their own message of assurance. "You're over-reacting, honey."

"Over-reacting? For God's sake. How can you say that?" There was a shock in her eyes now, and bewilderment. She shook her head. "You don't understand. You're not a woman so you don't understand. Nothing is more important for a woman than to be a mother. It's what we're here to do. Surely you see that?"

"I'm sorry, but I don't." He relaxed his hold on her so that she could breathe more easily. Then he unwound one arm and rubbed her back gently with a big hand. Still the blue eyes and the brown eyes talked to each other. He said seriously, almost gravely, "It would be nice to have some children, sure. But it's not what I married you for, Pam."

"What do you mean?" She looked bewildered again.

"I married you so that we could be together—approach the challenges and opportunities of life together. Why, we've hardly begun. You know the saying about holding a penny in front of your eye and blotting out the sun? That's what you're doing. Take the penny away, honey, and see the sun." He was caressing the back of her neck and shoulders now. He squeezed gently, kneading out the tension.

"But if I can't be a mother . . ."

"You can still be yourself, the wonderful, exciting woman I married. I married you because of you, Pamela."

"You really mean it?"

"Of course I do." He kissed her then, drawing her to him. He felt her relax and come alive in his embrace.

"William?"

"Yeah?"

"It's kind of crazy—eleven o'clock in the morning . . . but could we go back to bed?"

He grinned. "Just what I was thinking." He stooped, picked her up, carried her tender and clinging into the bedroom. He lowered her onto the bed, then stood looking at her for a moment. He knelt beside the bed, putting a hand over hers.

"One more thing," he said. "Doctors don't know everything. We may surprise old Roberts."

"I do love you," she said as she pulled him toward her.

* * *

Afterwards, when he was in hospital, with time to be more dispassionate, it did have its humorous aspect. Beresford smiled wryly. It was a classic scene, the stuff of novels and films. There was his wife, startled as a pheasant in a thicket. But while a pheasant is usually quick enough to escape, Julia was still in bed, half-raised on one shapely arm, her hair cascading around her neck and shoulders, her full lips just a little pinched with shock. He had not been due back for another three days. However, the deal to loan Sweden money for a new harbour system had fallen into place more quickly than he expected.

As a rule he kept in close touch with Julia while he was on a trip, but this time he did not. He flew to Gatwick, threw his suitcase into the boot of his Bentley, and pointed the old lady in the direction of his estate. Did he have a nudging suspicion that he would find his wife in a delicate situation? He was to ponder that later. But if such was indeed the case, he was nonetheless just as surprised as she was—let alone that prissy bastard Thistlewaite—when he walked into the bedroom, threw the switch and found the two of them in bed together. It is one thing to know something in theory, and he had known in theory for a long time that his wife was unfaithful. It is something else when the theory becomes fact before your eyes. Despite all the rumours that had circulated about his wife, he had never really faced up to her looseness or infidelity. Well, there was no avoiding it now!

"James darling, I didn't expect you . . ."

"So I see," he replied icily.

"For God's sake . . . James, old boy . . ." Thistlewaite was scared. So he should be, by God. He was climbing out of bed like a startled jackrabbit and struggling into a dressing gown.

Beresford stood there, not knowing what more to say. Usually he was not at a loss for a humorous remark. Now he could not even manage a quizzically raised eyebrow. He felt empty, like an abandoned house. There just was not anything to say. He had been living a lie. They had both been living a lie. Now it was thrust squarely in their faces.

"Oh God." He did, in the end, say that. After he had said it he simply turned and walked out of the room. The two lovers stared at each other, listening. Presently they heard the Bentley being revved fiercely, and a squeal of tires. Silence returned.

He swung west on the Guildford road, powerful beams stabbing the darkness. The road at this point ran fairly straight for a few miles. He pressed on the accelerator and the noble car responded instantly, moving ahead with a surge of power. He had the hood down, and the cool night air rushed past his ears. The car quivered like a living thing, putting out every ounce of power in response to his urgent command. Thus, like some omnipotent Greek charioteer, he rushed on, the road melting beneath him. The ground was a blur. The hedges were a blur. Julia had deceived him and betrayed him but there was solace in speed.

A small voice in Beresford told him to slow down, to wait, to forget, but he was in no mood to listen. At first he did not believe it when he saw, coming toward him in the distance, another pair of headlights. As sanity returned, his reflexes ground into gear, quite good still but not as good as when he was a fighter pilot and his chariot was a Spitfire. His foot bore down on the brake as he desperately geared down. The great Bentley made a valiant endeavour to obey, its engine, brakes, tires and chassis howling in dismay. For a moment everything seemed suspended in time. The headlights of the oncoming vehicle grew closer. He wrenched at the wheel and took the straining car to the left to avoid a collision on the narrow road. The Bentley, still doing fifty miles an hour, rammed through the hedge and came to a stop on its side in the middle of an empty field.

"How is he doing?"

"I think he may be on the point of waking, Doctor."

"Good. Give me a shout when he comes to."

Beresford heard the voices through a deep, dark mist. At first he questioned whether he had heard them at all, or if he was dreaming. Then a cool hand touched his forehead. There was no question but that the hand was real. It probed delicately but firmly, massaging the sides of his temples. He opened his eyes and saw a plump, cheerful face looking down at him. Brown eyes twinkled.

"My God, what happened?"

"There, there, love, there's nothing to worry about," the cheerful face said. "I'll be back in a minute." The nurse stepped out into the corridor, returning with a middle-aged man in a white coat who gazed at him sternly.

"Well, well, Mr. Beresford. You're a lucky man."

"What happened, Doctor? I remember a car coming towards me . . . Did I go off the road?"

"You did indeed. Finished up in the middle of a field. Anyway it looks like you're going to be all right. A few broken bones but nothing that won't mend."

Beresford felt the thick bandages around his chest and peered at his leg, which was also swathed and suspended in traction. "You've already done some work on me," he said. "Did it go all right?"

"Quite well, I would say," said the doctor. "With any luck you're through the worst of it. You've got a couple of fractures to the left leg and a broken collarbone, but that's all." The doctor had been studying a chart; now he hung it back on a hook at the end of the bed. "I'm Dr. Weatherby, by the way."

"Thank you, Dr. Weatherby. Thanks very much."

"Not at all. Just be a bit more careful next time. I gather you scared the daylights out of the other driver. Oh, and I believe the police want to have a word with you. When you feel up to it."

Beresford nodded faintly, closed his eyes and lay back on his pillow. His head throbbed like a steam engine. Other than that he was not too uncomfortable—except when he moved. God, what a mess. His car was wrecked. He would be out of commission for weeks. And what in heaven's name was he going to do about Julia?

The policeman arrived an hour later.

"Good evening, sir. I'm Police Constable Bowles," he said. "All right if I ask you a few questions then?" The young, red-faced constable perched on a chair beside his bed and opened his notebook.

"Oh you poor darling."

Beresford looked up to see Julia hovering over him, a small yellow purse in one hand and a package in the other. The smile on her face jarred him because it seemed too bright. She pulled the curtain around the bed, sat down beside him and gave him a kiss on the cheek.

"The police phoned me. I came at once," she said. She paused, looking at him anxiously out of her blue-green eyes. "I'm sorry, James," she whispered. "I know it's not enough, but I'm really sorry. Will you give me a chance to make it up to you?"

"Make it up?" He looked at her, frowning in surprise. He hadn't really known what to expect, but her words came as a shock nonetheless. "For Christ's sake do you think it's as easy as that? That you can hop into bed with people, people like Jimmy Thistlewaite"—a note of incredulity crept into his voice—"and then we just carry on, business as usual?" His jaw trembled slightly as he spoke.

"James." She put her purse and the package down on the bedside table. She was wearing the lime-green blouse he had bought for her in Paris that spring, and his favourite perfume. Her hands were clasped on her lap. "I've behaved terribly, I know. But I do love you. I really do." She reached out and took one of his hands. She looked contrite and provocative at the same time. My God, he thought to himself, how many times have I seen that look? That invitation? I've never been able to turn it down before. But now . . . somehow now it was different.

He withdrew his hand. It just didn't feel right. A compulsion of great force was building within him. "We can't sweep everything under the carpet," he said. "That's what we've done for as long as I can remember."

"You mean so much to me, James," she said. The provocative expression had faded. She looked bewildered, a little uncertain. She picked up the package she had brought. "I bought you something—two new Agatha Christies . . ." She laid the books down on the bed.

He knew he could put the moment of truth off no longer.

"Julia."

"Yes, darling?"

"I don't think it's going to work anymore."

Her eyes filled with tears. "Not going to work anymore?" she said. "What do you mean? You . . . you can't be serious. We need each other. The children need us." She looked at him desperately. "James, you love me, I know you do. Darling, it was wrong, I know it was, but it won't happen again. We can stay together. Oh God. Please. Say you'll forgive me."

He looked at her, seeing clearly for the first time who and what Julia was. He felt sorry for her, but he knew he could never love this woman again. He reached out, took her hand for a moment.

"It's no use," he said softly. Her hand, usually warm, was cold under his touch. "I've been thinking about things a lot. We've had some good times, Julia, but we don't fit together. I'll see you are comfortable and taken care of but I want a divorce."

She withdrew her hand. "My God," she said. "Oh my God."

The silence between them seemed to last an eternity. He could think of nothing more to say. The head nurse came in, all starch and efficiency. "Good afternoon," she said. "Sorry to interrupt but Dr. Weatherby is here and wants to make a check. He'll be along in a moment."

Julia rose, picked up her purse. "I'd better be going," she said in a hollow voice.

The head nurse checked his chart and began arranging some instruments by the side of the bed.

"Julia . . ." He wanted to say something more. But she had turned and was walking toward the exit.

Doubts rose up and plagued him but something within him insisted that he had done what needed to be done. There was no real basis for an agreement between them and probably never had been. Beresford knew that the reason he had not met the issue before was simply that he had not wanted to meet it. Julia's charms had been more important. Maintaining the fiction of a successful marriage had been important too. But better, he thought grimly as Dr. Weatherby took his wrist and began checking his pulse, to lose these things than to continue living a lie. At least he would stand on his own two feet now.

"How's it going, old chap?" Dr. Weatherby cocked his head a little on one side as he put the question.

Beresford smiled. "Not too bad," he said. "When are you going to let me out of here?"

Chapter XII

1956

Congressman William Kent welcomed the two visitors into his office. His aide sat to one side, doing his best to appear relaxed and confident. Kent noticed his discomfort and chuckled to himself. He could guess the reason.

The two visitors wasted no time getting to the point. "I think you know why we are here, Congressman," said the first, aggressively. Walter Page was chairman of the hospital committee which had been campaigning lately for a new hospital for Burningside, in Kent's home state. He was a short, bulky man with a red face. "To be blunt about it, sir, my committee is disgusted by your letter," he said. "I don't think you realize how much support our campaign has. Mrs. Byers and I decided we owe it to our community and our state to have a personal interview with you."

He sat scowling with displeasure. Mrs. Byers leaned forward. She was a woman of about forty, Kent guessed; brisk, attractive, with a smile that could win her a lot of votes if she ever went into politics.

"Congressman Kent, I know that you are trying to be fair and objective in this matter," she said pleasantly, "and I appreciate that. Indeed, I applaud the fact that you don't automatically support a project just because it is based in your own home state." She smiled modestly. "But while I applaud your approach, I must question the basis upon which you have arrived at your decision. You mentioned in your letter that you feel Alaska's need for a new mental hospital is greater than our own. Believe me, we have made a very thorough study and analysis. The need for a new facility for Burningside is urgent and well documented. That is why we are here today to ask you personally for your support."

She sat back, gazing at Kent with a warmth that—his aide guessed wryly—was probably not entirely phony. The Congressman was a handsome brute and that was a fact. All the same his stance in this case was no way to win friends or influence people. It might win him friends in Alaska but what use was that? Well, he'd done all he could. Given it to him straight. "Bill, it's political suicide," he had said. "No one goes against powerful local interests to help another state. You can be sure your Alaskan allies won't return the favour." What more could he do? All the same he didn't like to see Kent making such a mistake. He liked and respected the big man from New England more than most political figures he knew.

"Mrs. Byers, Colonel Page, I appreciate very much your coming to Washington to discuss this matter," said Kent, leaning his elbows on his desk and looking at each in turn. "I want you to know however that I've already given it exhaustive study. Tony here will tell you. We've gone over more reports and studies and projections for both proposals than you could imagine. Any way you look at it there's just no question which project is the most urgent. My decision is simply based on priority. I have no choice but to vote in favour of Alaska."

"In that case, sir, I have only one thing to say to you," Walter Page shouted, jumping to his feet. "You're an idiot! Here, take a look at these signatures . . ." He threw a small folder down on Kent's desk and stood, his face flushed beet red, his outstretched arm quivering. "There, sir, take a look at that. Twenty thousand people from your own state who support the campaign for a new Burningside Hospital. I'll tell you this much, sir, they aren't going to like this at all. It's . . . it's . . ." He was so angry he could hardly speak. "It's a slap in the face to all those who elected you. They won't forget, sir, they won't forget."

"Colonel Page . . ." Kent's aide had some notion about trying to defuse the situation.

"Please, Colonel Page, let's relax a little, shall we?" Mrs. Byers was still keeping her smile, though it was becoming a little ragged at the edges. There was no mistaking the note of authority in her voice, however. It stopped her colleague in his tracks and he sat down, grumbling. Mrs. Byers looked at Kent, a hint of frostiness in her eyes. "We're not going to get anywhere by becoming emotional," she said. "As I say, Mr. Kent, you have every right to take an objective view based on the merits of the situation. However, it is also true, as my colleague suggests, that you were elected to represent a certain area—a certain sector of the population. Obviously you have a particular responsibility to them. I hope you're not forgetting that?" Her words, spoken coolly with just the barest hint of anger, had much more impact than her colleague's outburst. Kent felt a moment of self-doubt. Mrs. Byers sensed her advantage. She opened the slim briefcase on her knees and took out a file of papers which she placed on the desk in front of Kent.

"This is a summary of all our findings to this point," she remarked. "Please, please go over the points very carefully. This is such an important matter for us."

"I will indeed, Mrs. Byers. Thank you."

"And take a look at those signatures, sir. Your own constituents. What good are votes going to do you up in Alaska, eh?" Page snorted, reasserting himself.

"Let me say just one thing." Kent paused, pondering his choice of words. "Obviously the hospital you propose is going to be needed at some point and you and your colleagues are to be commended most strongly for the work you have put into this project. Right now it appears that Alaska's need is imperative—something that simply cannot wait. But I want you to know that when the time comes I will fight for a new Burningside Hospital with everything I have."

"That's a nice thought, Mr. Congressman. But it doesn't help us now, does it?" Mrs. Byers had turned icy. There was no vestige of a smile on her face anymore. Kent frowned. The flicker of doubt was still there, but he was not going to give in to it.

"I can only say that the view of experts, whom I have to trust, is that with a fairly modest addition in two or three years, the existing Burningside Hospital should be adequate for another five to ten years," he said doggedly. "On the other hand Alaska's need is acute. How can I ignore that or put it in jeopardy?"

His aide whistled to himself. He had been around Congress a good many years. It wasn't very common for a politician to stand up against strong local pressure groups on a point of principle. It did happen, of course. He recalled an emotional moment on the House floor when a Democratic Congressman from Louisiana rose up to support the voting rights bill despite strong adverse opinion back home. Then there was the Senator from Idaho who led a fight for a wilderness bill even though it was anathema to powerful lumber and mining interests in his home state. Both of them could have ducked, just like Kent could have ducked this one.

"Walter, we are wasting our breath," said Mrs. Byers, a pink spot the size of a quarter showing clearly on each cheek. "I think it is time to go."

"Absolutely. Come on, my dear." The colonel rose, scowling fiercely in Kent's direction. "You'll regret this," he said threateningly as they walked out of the office. Their footsteps echoed down the marble-floored corridor.

"Whew."

"I'll say," said the aide.

"I guess there's a few people who won't be voting for me next year."

At another time, or with another person, the aide would have been tempted to say, "I told you so." But instead he asked, "How about a beer?"

Kent nodded gratefully. "Good idea," he said. "I'll meet you at the Rotunda. I want to phone Pam first."

When his aide had left, Kent picked up the phone and dialled a long-distance number.

"Hello, Pam?"

"Darling, where are you?"

"In my office. Walter Page and Mrs. Byers came to see me about the new hospital."

"Was it bad?"

"Pretty bad. How's everything?"

"Just fine, darling. Did you stick to your guns?"

"Yeah. It's going to cost me votes, but what the heck. I really think I'm right."

She sensed the concern in his voice.

"I know you are. And that's the only thing that matters, Bill."

"Page nearly had a heart attack. They gave me a petition with 20,000 names in favour of the new hospital for Burningside."

"So what? The Federal Studies clearly show the priority is in Alaska. You had no choice."

"Thanks, honey. It's been good talking to you. I'll be home on the Saturday morning flight. See you then."

"Bye, darling. I love you."

Kent put the phone down and grinned. The flickerings of doubt evaporated. He whistled softly, as he made his way to the Rotunda.

* * *

The smooth-tongued Malenkov began his ploy. "True, the Congress is going smoothly," he said. "But perhaps it is going too smoothly? After all, we have not yet dealt with the findings of Comrade Pospelov concerning the Stalin years."

Nikita Sergeyevich Khrushchev, the First Secretary of the Communist Party of the Union of Soviet Socialist Republics, felt a twinge of pain in his liver, always a sign he was under tension. He did not speak. Instead, he looked up at the Cossack horseman who, sabre raised, charged across a huge Susnov canvas.

Anastas Mikoyan spoke. "Comrade Yegor is correct. We cannot ignore this matter. It must be met with resolution. The Party must be reminded in no uncertain terms that Stalin is dead and the Praesidium is firmly in control." Mikoyan, the supreme survivor of them all, looked around the small circle with his usual dour expression.

With only a few more days to go before the Twentieth Party Congress came to a conclusion, the Praesidium was gathered in a meeting room off the main hall of the Kremlin. Khrushchev knew that his goal of complete power was close, like a ripe peach. But he also knew instinctively that what happened in this innocuous little hour between sessions was crucial to his bid for supremacy. He did not dare lose sight of the fact that Malenkov was still a formidable opponent.

Bulganin, Khrushchev's trusty stalking-horse, sensed the fierce undertow. He tried in his usual cautious way to help. "It will reflect on the prestige of our party and our country if we bring out the findings of the Pospelov commission," he said reasonably, his goatee dancing as he spoke. "You won't be able to keep what you say secret. The whole world will hear about the abuses of power under Stalin and then the finger will point directly at us. People will say we should have spoken up or done something to stop it."

Yegor Malenkov smiled, a hint of self-satisfaction on his pudgy face as he played the role of the man of principle. "Can we allow fear of the consequences to prevent us from doing what we know is right?" he asked smoothly. "Thanks to Comrade Pospelov and his enquiry we know that appalling crimes were committed under Stalin. Hundreds of thousands of innocent people are still imprisoned in the camps. Loyal party members were shot or imprisoned. Monstrous abuses were perpetrated against innocent people devoted to the Party, to the Revolution, to the ideals of Lenin." He paused, turned his gaze directly to the First Secretary. "We have no choice but to let the truth come out. I suggest, Comrade Khruschev, that as First Secretary you are the logical one to bear the news."

The room was quiet as Malenkov played his master card, then sat back smugly in his chair. Bastard, the First Secretary thought as his mind raced over the options open to him. Outmanoeuvred and outvoted the previous year, when he had been forced to relinquish the Premiership on grounds of "inexperience," Malenkov had obviously not given up his ambition to take the top spot in the Party for himself. The others, smelling blood, moved in quickly.

"An excellent suggestion," said Molotov. "Who better than the First Secretary to tell the Party the truth?"

"It is three years since our former leader died and yet still we live under his shadow, afraid to assert ourselves," said Kaganovich in his thick Ukrainian Jewish accent. "I agree with

Comrades Malenkov and Mikoyan. We must show the Party, and the people, that we are the leaders and that a new chapter in the history of our great country has begun. Certainly no one is better suited to present the necessary facts and information than the First Secretary."

The tension in the room increased unbearably. You all think there's going to be an outcry and people will turn on me because I dared to expose our great leader, Stalin, Khrushchev thought grimly. A bold idea came to him, burgeoning in his cunning peasant's brain. But he needed more time. A few more moments to think before he committed himself.

"No one should doubt," the First Secretary began, "my concern that the Party be informed of the truth. After all, it was I who made the original proposal that we investigate what happened under Stalin. I have been tormented by the thought that the Congress will end and these terrible abuses of power will remain on our consciences, festering like a boil on the backside." He chuckled, then added in his most reasonable tone, "But I respectfully submit that the most appropriate person to deliver the address is Comrade Pospelov himself. After all, he was the chairman of the commission that conducted the investigation."

"Nyet, nyet. You must make the speech." Three or four voices spoke as one.

He was beginning to enjoy himself. The notion that had sprung up in his mind looked better the more he studied it. He would play with these crooks a little more and then he would turn the tables on them. It was a gamble, yes, but he had gambled before and won. What was it the English said? "Nothing venture, nothing win." Yes. He was sure now.

"But comrades, I already delivered my General Report without saying a word about Pospelov's findings. How can I get up now and tell the Party all about them?" he asked. "No, I refuse."

Malenkov leapt in shrewdly. "If Pospelov, another Central Committee Secretary, delivers the speech, it will make people wonder. 'Why didn't Khrushchev say anything about this business in his report?' they will ask. 'Why is Pospelov bringing up such an important matter now? How could Khrushchev not have known? Or if he knew, how could he not have placed any importance on it?'"

The First Secretary listened attentively as the others supported Malenkov.

"Yegor is right," said Kaganovich. "If you don't give the speech, it will look as if we are divided."

"The one thing we wish to avoid," concurred Molotov.

Finally, with a show of reluctance, Khrushchev acceded.

"Perhaps you are right," he said. "Perhaps I am the one who should bring this matter before the Party. We will need to arrange a closed session of the Congress. I will instruct Comrade Pospelov to turn his report into a speech." He raised himself from the chair. When Bulganin walked over, looking worried, he poked him playfully in the belly with a stubby forefinger and joked with him. Yes, it was a gamble all right, but the odds were reasonable. And if it came off, if the process of "de-Stalinization" which he would initiate caught the imagination of the Party and the country, then he, Nikita Khrushchev, would get the credit. Yes, he thought to himself. It would seem as if he was the one man who had dared to speak out!

In a hall so quiet that you could have heard a fly buzzing, Nikita Khrushchev stepped to the front of the podium.

"Comrades!" he began. "In the report of the Central Committee of the Party at the Twentieth Congress, in a number of speeches . . . much has been said about the cult of the individual and about its harmful consequences. After Stalin's death the Central Committee began to implement a policy of explaining concisely and consistently that it is impermissible and foreign to the spirit of Marxism-Leninism to elevate one person, to transform him into a superman possessing supernatural characteristics akin to those of a god. Such a man supposedly knows everything, sees everything, thinks for everyone, can do anything, is infallible in his behaviour. Such a belief about a man, and specifically about Stalin, was cultivated among us for many years.

". . . We are concerned with a question which has immense importance for the Party now and for the future, with how the cult of the person of Stalin has been gradually growing, the cult which became at a certain specific stage the source of a whole series of exceedingly serious and grave perversions of Party principles, of Party democracy, of revolutionary legality . . . .

"Because of the fact that not all as yet realize the practical consequences resulting from the cult of the individual, the great harm caused by the violation of the principle of collective direction of the Party, and because of the accumulation of immense and limitless power in the hands of one person, the Central Committee of the Party considers it absolutely necessary to make the material pertaining to this matter available to the Twentieth Congress of the Communist Party of the Soviet Union . . . ."

By the time he finished, everyone realized that a time of "thaw" was about to begin, following the terrible excesses of the Stalinist era.

"I think it's good, Grigori. Very good," said his old school friend, Leonid Yaklovlev. "You've done a fine job—and your first attempt at a book, too. It's remarkable." Yaklovlev stopped speaking, as if afraid he might say too much. He flicked a little speck of dust off the sleeve of his Western-cut suit. Both men paused awkwardly for a few moments.

"So you have read it, Leonid?"

"Oh yes."

But, Grigori realized, his old friend was avoiding looking at him directly. When he was not flicking specks of dust off his fine suit he was examining his fingernails or the portrait of his family that sat on his desk.

"The letter just said that your company was sorry but it could not accept the book because of other commitments. You understand I don't want to be a nuisance, Leonid. I accept the decision. I just thought you might be able to give me a suggestion or two. Perhaps the names of some other people I could try?"

"Ah yes. Yes, of course." Yaklovlev stole a glance in his direction. As their eyes met, Grigori saw the fear clearly and unmistakably. "Yes, if I can help, I certainly will. You must understand, Grigori, that the book is . . . what shall I say? . . . daring? a little controversial? Mind you, I think we need more young writers like yourself and Voznesensky and others. It's wonderful. But as a publisher one has to balance the idealistic with the practical, you understand. And unfortunately, we do have more books waiting to be published already than we can really handle."

"I understand." The publishing house where Leonid worked prospered on tales of heroic tractor drivers and factory workers, along with cold-war spy stories. *Lyubimov, Agent for the KGB* had sold something approaching half a million copies, he had heard. In a way, he hadn't expected Leonid Yaklovlev to be too interested in *Sergeant Mihailovich*. But it had been a place to start.

Now that he felt the interview was at least halfway through and over the hump, Yaklovlev relaxed a little. He walked over to a cocktail cabinet. "A drink, Grigori? For old time's sake?" He poured the vodka, gave a glass to Grigori. They tossed their glasses back.

"We live in difficult times, Grigori, difficult times." He settled back in his comfortable padded chair. "Even though Comrade Khrushchev has taken a bold step and shown the excesses of the Stalin era for what they are, the Hungarian revolt shows that we cannot afford to go to another extreme. The people are not ready for it. Open the gates too wide and there would be anarchy. It could destroy everything we've worked for so far. As a responsible citizen I have to tread a very delicate line . . . often turning down material which I personally sympathize with. What, I ask myself, will be its effect on the masses? Will it have a creative influence on that larger scale? Take your book for instance . . ." Yaklovlev suddenly was feeling more confident. "It's a good story. No doubt about it. But could it stimulate a cult of the individual? a rebellious attitude toward authority? I have to ask myself such questions, Grigori, and set aside personal feelings in favour of the truth." He paused, blinked his pale eyes in Grigori's direction. "You do understand, don't you?" he asked anxiously. "It's nothing personal, you see."

"Yes, I understand," said Grigori slowly, nodding his head. "But it's not the way you used to talk when we were at school, Leonid." Grigori remembered Leonid Yaklovlev. As a youngster, he had been a lot of fun. The two of them had got into all kinds of scrapes together. Now he relied on lengthy rationalizations to explain why he didn't want to stick his neck out. Grigori, who had seen many men cowed and broken in the camps—while others prevailed—reflected sorrowfully that a man could be cowed and broken even in the midst of luxury and comfort. It must, he decided, have to do with all the little choices that one made as the years went by, determining the ultimate nature of a person's character.

"Ah, schooldays. The best years of our life, eh, Grigori?" Yaklovlev had not perceived the gibe in his remark, or else chose to ignore it. Well, whichever way it was, Grigori thought, he had ended up a nonentity. But what a shame it was. He remembered a time when the two of them found a raft and pushed out into the broad stream of the Oka River near Ryazan. They had been proceeding in fine style, extremely pleased with themselves, until Leonid lost their makeshift paddle and they drifted into the path of an oncoming barge. They had survived that scrape, by luck and the skin of their teeth. But surviving life was something different. And mastering life? Something different again.

As he looked at his old school chum, Grigori saw how he had become a slave to conformity and bureaucracy. He saw how precious the little material comforts had become to him, and how his whole life revolved around them. He thought of his own days of comfort, and how easily they had been shattered. He felt a sudden compassion. Who was he to sit in judgment on this man? In his own way, perhaps Yaklovlev had had as tough and difficult a time keeping his soul alive outside the camps as he had had inside. And if Leonid had not succeeded, well that was between him and his creator. A smile lit Grigori's weatherbeaten face. He felt a warm glow of love reach out and enfold the other man. The past, even the past of five minutes back, did not matter anymore.

"Oh my dear friend," Yaklovlev exclaimed. "What has become of us?" Suddenly the two men were out of their chairs and hugging each other, breaking through the years of separation and the years in which their lives had taken such different, contrary paths. "I hope you can get your book published, Grigori, really I do," Yaklovlev said as they drew apart. He was desperately massaging the palm of his left hand with his right thumb as if seeking to expunge some hidden pain or guilt.

"It's all right, Leonid. I understand, really."

"Even though Khrushchev seems to be letting things soften a little, we are still very restricted. I have my family to think of, too, Grigori."

"Of course."

"And you do understand that our lists really are full. People in authority keep coming to me and saying I must publish this or I must publish that. Stories about a train driver in Murmansk or a peasant in Kazakhstan or a brave KGB man outfoxing the Americans. My life is not my own, Grigori, and that is a fact. But I tell you what." His face brightened. "I will speak to my friend Boris Polyansky. I will tell him about your book and say that I recommend it. He is a publisher too, a brilliant man. He has more freedom than me because of his connections. If he likes the book he may be able to do something for you."

"Thank you, I really appreciate it."

"Not at all, not at all. I hope he likes it. How is your mother?"

"She is fine."

"A wonderful woman. Wonderful. And what about your personal life? It is time you got married."

"Not yet."

Leonid put an arm around his shoulder as he walked him to the door of his office.

"Poor man, you must have lost a lot of weight in the camps. It's good to have you back, and that's a fact. We must get together for dinner sometime."

"Yes, we must."

"Well, good-bye, old friend. I'll be in touch with Polyansky."

"Good-bye, Leonid."

Outside on Gorky Street the air was crisp. Grigori buttoned up his overcoat and headed toward his mother's apartment. He was glad about the cold. It helped cleanse him of the atmosphere of fear that had pervaded the office of his friend.

Chapter XIII

1957

"Someone's after my ass, Joe."

Earl Wilson, director of the Federal Development Agency of the United States Government, was angry. And also a touch scared.

"What's up?" the other man asked. He had the smooth off-hand manner of someone who costs big money in Washington but gets results.

Earl Wilson looked around the lounge of the hotel for a moment and drew his chair closer. "This goddam committee that keeps an eye on 'Project Highrise,'" he said. "It's getting too damn curious all of a sudden. They've heard rumours about my kickback on the construction bids. I got wind of it three days ago through one of my deputies, Chuck Benson."

"Chuck's a good boy."

"Damn right. Anyway, one of his assistants got asked a bunch of fool questions and had to pull some files."

"So the subcommittee is getting curious. Let's see. There was a change, wasn't there? Who's in charge of it now?"

"Congressman Kent. Big sonofabitch from New England."

"I know him."

"Had any dealings with him?"

"No. I just know him by reputation. He's supposed to be a straight shooter."

"Just my goddam luck."

Earl Wilson brooded over his double martini, a petulant expression on his handsome, florid face.

"I've got to do something, Joe."

"What do you have in mind?"

"I need to find some dirt to trade with. You know as well as I do that no one is really straight. This sonofabitch must have something going on the side somewhere."

The other man pursed his lips, smoothed his silver hair with a well-manicured hand. "Finding dirt" was not a commonly used expression in the vocabulary of Joseph R. Charlesworth, senior partner of Charlesworth and Stevens, attorneys-at-law. He preferred to think of this aspect of his profession as "creating personality profiles."

"Maybe so. But I don't think I'd count on it."

"Yeah?" Wilson looked incredulous.

"From what I have heard, Congressman Kent is an unusual man. People call him a sort of modern-day Abraham Lincoln, except that he is smoother and bigger. You wouldn't want to tangle with him, Earl."

"I'm not a pussycat. I'll push his teeth down his throat."

Charlesworth smiled, but kept his thought to himself. The idea of pushing Kent's teeth down his throat was amusing.

"He was with the OSS in the war. You know, blowing up dams, knifing German soldiers, that kind of thing?" Charlesworth spoke casually.

Wilson ignored the remarks.

"You really think he's clean?" he asked.

"I'll look into the matter more closely, but that's my impression. I'll be surprised if we come up with anything. He once voted against a hospital in his own state because he thought a similar project for Alaska had more priority."

"Sonofabitch. And he still got voted back in?"

The lawyer took a plum-coloured handkerchief from his

pocket and polished his glasses. When he had replaced them on his nose he continued. "He puts principles first but he is also clever. It's a combination that his constituents seem to like."

"Principles hell," Wilson snorted. "Everyone's got a weak point. I want you to get busy and find it. I don't care what it costs. This guy could ruin me."

Charlesworth finished his highball. "Very well. We'll do a profile. But as I say, I wouldn't count on anything."

"Yeah? You're really serious, for chrissake." Earl Wilson lost his petulant expression and looked worried. Joe Charlesworth usually knew what he was talking about. He leaned forward in his chair, one fist clenched and resting on the table. His voice was hard. "There's more than one way to skin a cat. If you can't find anything on this guy we'll have to work out something else. I'm not going down the tube on this one, though. There's too damn much at stake."

"What sort of 'something else,' Earl?" Charlesworth asked.

Wilson smiled. An idea had occurred to him. The more he thought about it the more he liked it. "How about we say he's a queer?"

Charlesworth looked thoughtful.

"It fixed Senator Irvine good, didn't it?" Wilson continued. "Poor sucker hardly dared sneeze after the word got around."

The silver-haired man steepled his fingers and tapped them on his chin.

"You may have a thought there. It's the one thing that might stop him. Slow him down, anyway," he said.

"Damn right. Irvine never even fought it. You know that?"

"It might work, Earl."

"Damn right it would work. As soon as we've got him, we can tell him we'll lay off if he calls off his investigation."

"What do you want me to do?"

"Look for the dirt first. But if that's no go then get someone to set up the smear. And I don't have much time, Joe."

"It's going to cost you, Earl. I will need to get a research assistant to look after the details."

"The hell with the cost. Who you got in mind?"

"There's a man called Gucci who might take it on. He's done some work for me before. He is tough but very discreet."

"Just what we want." Wilson looked positively cheerful.

"I'll proceed with the matter immediately, then."

"Thanks, Joe. I'll make it worth your while."

The attorney winced. He did not like discussing remuneration. "I've always been very happy with the financial end of our friendship," he said.

"I bet you have, you old bullshitter. Hey, how did you like that broad I got for you last weekend?"

Joseph R. Charlesworth looked even more pained than before. The florid-faced man laughed, clapped him on the shoulder as they made their way out of the lounge. "You're all right, Joe," he said. He was still chuckling as they emerged onto the street.

By the end of the next day Joseph R. Charlesworth was a very troubled man. It is one thing to have problems come up in one's business affairs—he was continually having to deal with difficult issues in his law practice—or even in more difficult situations like "finding dirt," as Wilson called it. It is something else, however, when one's life is abruptly threatened. And that had happened to him that morning. After his meeting with Wilson he had flown to New York expecting to have a comfortable lunch with Gucci, during which he would bring up the plans to deal with Kent. He had planned to be back in Washington by five. Well, he was back in Washington all right, but the lunch had been far from comfortable. After twenty minutes with Gucci he felt like he was caught between a rock and a hard place with a truckload of gravel about to drop on his head. It had never occurred to him that there might be a connection between Gucci and Kent.

He tried Wilson's number for the fifth time. He sat in his elegant office sliding a silver ashtray round and round in a circle, saying impatiently, "Come on, Earl, come on." The phone rang six or seven times. Finally someone picked it up. "Wilson here," said an angry and impatient voice.

"Earl? I've been trying to get you for fifteen minutes."

"Phone's been going crazy. What do you want, Joe? I'm pretty busy right now." Wilson winked at his secretary on the sofa.

"I have to see you. It's urgent." Earl Wilson caught the worry behind the normally cool and urbane expression, and frowned.

"What's up, for chrissake?"

"I can't talk on the phone. It's about that matter we were discussing. We have a problem. A big one, Earl."

"The hell you say." He sat upright in his chair, his jaw shut tight and eyes narrowed. He looked at his watch. "No way I can make it tonight, Joe. I have a meeting in an hour. It'll have to be in the morning. Ten o'clock okay?"

"If it's the best you can do . . ." The other man sounded a bit doubtful. "Could you come to my office?"

"Sure. Relax, Joe, it'll keep till the morning."

"I hope so. I'll see you at ten then."

Wilson put the receiver down, still frowning. He looked at the redhead and walked over to the sofa. She raised an eyebrow at him. He smiled. The feeling of worry he had picked up from Charlesworth dissolved.

"We don't have much time, baby," he said.

It was just past eleven that evening when Earl Wilson returned to his apartment after speaking to the National Society of Professional Engineers about "Project Highrise." It was time to relax, mix himself a drink and catch a little action on the tube. His first intimation that something was wrong came when he opened the door of the apartment and switched on the light. He became aware of a subtle scent. Was it some kind of men's cologne? What in hell was going on? He shut the door, looked around, then gasped in surprise. A dark-haired man was sitting at the small bar adjacent to the living room. He swivelled toward him on the stool and smiled, showing strong, white teeth.

"Mr. Wilson?"

"Who the hell are you? What are you doing in my apartment?" The florid-faced man put as much bluster as he could into the words but there was a knot of fear inside his belly. Could this have anything to do with Charlesworth's phone call?

"You don't know me, Mr. Wilson. Take your coat off and relax, huh? Here, I'll fix some drinks." The intruder went and busied himself behind the counter. "There you are, Mr. Wilson," he said, handing him a scotch and soda. "I just want to have a little chat." He sat down again at the bar.

"How the hell did you get in here?" Wilson said. He stood uncertainly in the middle of the room. It didn't seem the guy wanted to rob him, but the whole thing was damn strange. Should he try to call the police? It didn't seem wise just yet.

The other man ignored his question. He had stopped smiling now and was gazing at Wilson intently with dark, nearly black, eyes. Despite himself, Wilson flicked a glance at the telephone sitting on a small table a few feet away.

"I wouldn't even think of it," the other man murmured. His voice was still casual, but there was an edge to it that made the knot in Wilson's stomach tighten several turns. He had dealt with many men. Most of them had their weaknesses, one way or another. They could be read by someone who knew human nature, and Earl Wilson knew human nature. But this person was different. Suddenly Wilson knew what the difference was. He was one of those guys that killed people. Mafia. Cosa Nostra. Whatever the hell name they used. Devious though he was, Earl Wilson still had a certain basic respect for what he would have called "law and order." Indeed, if someone had called him a crook he would have been very offended. But this smooth-faced sonofabitch who'd broken into his apartment and helped himself to his liquor was a cat from a different jungle who went by his own rules. Wilson knew it. And he was afraid.

"Please, mister . . . Who are you and what do you want?" he asked, his customary arrogance punctured like a balloon.

"Good. I like politeness." He was mocking him now. "Well, I'll tell you. My name is Gucci. Frank Gucci. Does that mean anything?" The stranger finished his drink, reached for the bottle of Haig and Haig and poured himself a generous refill, ignoring Wilson's empty glass.

Wilson looked at him, puzzled. "Yeah. But I . . . I don't understand. Did Charlesworth see you?"

"Yes. He saw me this afternoon, the elegant creep. Nice little scheme you dreamed up."

"What did you think?" Wilson tried to inject a note of confidence into his expression but failed rather dismally.

"What did I think?" The younger man leapt from his stool and seized the front of Wilson's shirt by the collar. "Well it's this way, fatso." He pulled the florid face towards him, holding it just a few inches from his own. Wilson was painfully aware of the whipcord strength of the man's arms. His hand was like a vice, half-throttling him as it made a twist, still holding the front of his collar. "This guy you want to set up happens to be a friend of mine, see?" Wilson felt his head being shaken back and forth. A terrible pain pressed down on top of his skull. A mist swam over his eyes. He struggled for breath. The man released his grip a small fraction, and Wilson took several painful gulps of air.

"Friend?" he managed to croak.

"Right." The other man looked at him speculatively. "A personal friend. Congressman Bill Kent and I go back a long way together. I don't want to hear any bullshit about him, understand? If I do I will come back to see you." Gucci slapped him viciously across the face with the back of his hand. Wilson cried out in pain, cringed pathetically away from his tormentor, and sat on the sofa.

"Understand?"

Earl Wilson nodded. He felt the taste of blood in his mouth.

Gucci smiled.

"Good. Don't bother to get up. I'll let myself out."

He walked to the door, then paused, looking back. Wilson had in fact risen from the sofa and taken a hesitant step toward the telephone. Their eyes met. Wilson backed against the wall. He stared at Gucci, eyes filled with pain and hate.

"One more point," said Gucci casually. His arm flicked forward and he released the slim, pearl-handled throwing knife. It sped across the room and stuck quivering in the wall an inch from Wilson's left ear.

Gucci walked over and retrieved the knife, replacing it carefully in the sheath strapped to the back of his leg. Earl Wilson stood immobile, as if turned to stone. Only his lips moved, as if uttering a prayer. Suddenly his eyes closed and he fainted. He slid slowly to the floor and collapsed. Gucci took his pulse, nodded.

"I think you got the point," he said. "See you around, fatso."

* * *

Grigori reached for the bottle that stood on his cheap table and took another swallow. The room was as cheerless as a cell, with its dingy nondescript wallpaper, ancient bedstead and a low-powered bulb in the ceiling. God knows why he had chosen this place, except that rooms were hard to find and it was at a rent that he could afford. He had to get out of his mother's place when he began going down. It had been too hard on both of them.

Funny how the sense of despair had crept up on him. At work, when he could keep busy handling the boxes and heavy containers at the warehouse, it was not so bad. He enjoyed the companionship of the other workers and the banter, even though he did not feel close to any of them. They were all good, solid working types, wrapped up in their own everyday worlds. They liked to talk about women, sport and drinking. But none of them had been in the camps, which might have provided a bridge for a closer communion.

It was when Grigori returned home to his room at night that the feeling of despair hit him most hard. For four years now he had been trying to get his book published. He felt as if the vision he had touched in the camps was being slowly extinguished. How ironic, he thought to himself, that it was being extinguished in the outside world, when it had grown and flourished in the harsh environment of Ust-Ulenov.

In his book, he had tried to portray the evils and excesses of the war and of the camps, but also the many fine qualities of character which he had seen exhibited during those difficult years. He had suggested that there was an untapped source of greatness within each individual which, if released, could enrich and perhaps transform society. Yet now even he seemed unable to release that source.

"I'm sorry, Antoniev," one highly placed editor had told him—it was Polyansky, the contact of Yaklovlev's—"but we have to be very careful. I like your story. It's quite good. But it could be construed as contributing to the cult of the individual. And even though Comrade Khrushchev has gone so far as to publicly denounce Stalin, I'm not so sure that the Party or the people for that matter would be ready for the things that you reveal about the camps. Why not come up with something safer and more acceptable? More traditional. You have the talent. You could write a splendid story about a young tractor driver who finds solace for his romantic heartache in his work. Or about a woman factory worker who wants to improve the efficiency at her plant but is victimized by a lazy, dissolute supervisor. Do you see what I mean? Give me a story along this line and I can almost guarantee that I could get it published for you."

One evening at eight o'clock there was a knock on the door of his room. He had fallen asleep, and between that and the vodka it took him a few moments to clear his head. The knock came again. "All right," he growled, "I'm coming." He swung himself off the bed and went to the door. His steps were unsteady. He pulled the door open and peered out. He had forgotten to shave that day. With his dishevelled hair, dirty shirt and bleary, bloodshot eyes, he was not an attractive sight. At first he could not believe who was standing in the doorway.

"Andropovich? It can't be you."

"It is, old friend." The other man threw his arms around Grigori Antoniev, and they hugged ecstatically.

"I cannot believe it. Yevgeny Andropovich. Is it really you?" Grigori felt his eyes moistening. What did it matter? He straightened himself up, looked the other man in the eye. "I am sorry that you do not see me at my best," he said.

Andropovich smiled. "It is enough to see you again," he said. "May I come in?"

"Of course, of course. Please, take a seat." Grigori hurriedly drew a chair forward for his friend.

"How did you find me?" he asked. "How did you know I was here?"

"Your mother told me," said his friend. "She heard that I had moved to Moscow from Leningrad and searched half the city to find me. She is very worried about you. But you know that, eh?" Andropovich looked at him closely.

Grigori nodded. "I know," he said. He went to a cupboard and opened it. It was almost empty. He looked at his friend over his shoulder. "Can I offer you something?" he asked. "I have a little sausage here."

"No thank you, Grigori," the other said. "I am not hungry.

I do not wish to be inquisitive, my friend. But your mother thinks you have become discouraged because you could not get your book published. Is it true?"

"Yes. I suppose it is," sighed Grigori. He sat down heavily, his face creased with pain. "I have never been in this state before. I do not understand it. But I do not seem to be able to get out of it. I think it is just that I reached too high. I must give up some of these silly dreams that I have had."

"Nonsense, my friend."

"What did you say?" Grigori looked startled.

"I said nonsense."

"What do you mean?"

"I have read your manuscript. Your mother brought it to me. It is excellent, Grigori. You tell a good story, and you touch on matters that are important. You must never give up. Did we not agree on that in the camps?"

"Yes, we did. But the fact is that no one is willing to publish it."

"That is not true."

"What do you mean 'not true'?" Grigori looked angry and perplexed.

"I am prepared to publish your book."

"You?" Grigori was now thoroughly confused.

"Aha. I see I have your interest. Relax a little, my earnest friend, and I will explain."

Andropovich looked pleased with himself. He hummed a little tune under his breath as he took his pipe from his jacket and filled it. His fingers moved delicately. He was a man of contradictions, Yevgeny Andropovich. His eyes were soft, like a child's, but his jaw was strong. The overall impression was one of calmness and contentment. Very rarely had anyone seen Andropovich become angry in the camps.

"So, Grigori," he said when he had finished lighting his pipe. "I am here partly because I wished to see you again, yes. But I am also here because I have a proposition to make."

"A proposition?" Grigori could not help interrupting, though he was sorry when he saw the small frown on his friend's face.

"Yes. Please be quiet while I finish. Imagine my surprise, Grigori. I was teaching a class of philosophy students at my university when I received word that a small delegation from Moscow had travelled all the way down to see me. I finished my class. I do not like to be rushed. I then invited them to my office. The head of the delegation was from the Department of Cultural Affairs. He told me that his department had been authorized to launch a new literary magazine to be called *New Horizon*. The purpose—this is what he said—is to encourage new forms of literary and cultural expression."

Andropovich paused for a few moments, and took some vigorous puffs on his pipe before continuing. "It appears that Comrade Khrushchev himself is behind the project," he went on. "He sees it as a vehicle through which he can continue his policies of de-Stalinization and encourage writers who are helpful to his aims. Anyway, to make a long story short they said I was one of a dozen candidates whom they were considering for the post of editor of this magazine. I had to travel to Moscow and be nice to a lot of dull people but I got the job, Grigori. I am now the editor of *New Horizon*. While I cannot promise anything, I intend to do all I can to have your book published in serial form. In fact, I have already spoken to a few people. Now. What do you think of that?"

Andropovich sat back in his chair, his face wreathed in self-satisfaction. He squinted at Grigori over the bowl of his battered old pipe. A cloud of blue smoke drifted up toward the ceiling.

Grigori felt almost light-headed. Life was so full of surprises. Just when everything seemed so hopeless, his friend Andropovich appeared—and with such an interesting offer. Could it be that there really was a design to it all? that everything he had been through had been necessary to bring him to this point? He felt himself relaxing inside for the first time in a long while.

"Thank you, Yevgeni," he said. "It is good of you to care so much."

"My God, what are friends for? Why did we go through so much together? As I say, I cannot make any promises, but your book is definitely worth publishing, and furthermore I believe it fits in with our new leader's purposes."

Andropovich stood up. He looked thoughtfully at Grigori. "I think, my friend," he said, "that you could use a good square meal. What do you think? Shall we go and find a place? I am hungry myself now."

Grigori nodded. They gathered their coats and clattered down the stairs into the street.

* * *

Pamela Kent stopped outside the bookstore. She was not due for her doctor's apppointment for another twenty minutes. This would be as good a place as anywhere to spend time. She walked inside. The bookshop was new, nicely lit and well laid out. A bored-looking young man wearing wire-rimmed spectacles sat behind the counter writing on a scratch pad. He looked up as she walked in, then suddenly seemed to stop being bored. He put the scratch pad down and stood up, smiling his darnedest. "Good afternoon, madam," he said eagerly, "may I help you in any way?" He had acne but it was a friendly face.

"I don't think so, thank you. May I just browse a little?"

"Of course, ma'am. Please let me know if you need any assistance." The boy kept on looking at her, his eyes nearly falling out of their sockets. She smiled, despite herself. "Thank you," she said, and began looking at the nearest bookcase. The assistant sat down again at his counter and made a show of going through a catalogue. From time to time he stole lingering glances at the dark-haired woman with whom he had just spoken. "Jeez. Wonder if she's a famous film star," he thought to himself.

Pamela moved idly down some shelves. One or two volumes attracted a mild interest. She withdrew them, leafed through a few pages, but soon replaced them. A book on dogs was more interesting—she and Bill were thinking of buying one—and she spent two or three minutes examining it. Holding it in her hand, she went on to a display table, where she noticed a book bearing the title *The Healing of the Nations*. Attracted to it, she picked up a copy. It was by a Dr. Lionel Denton and there was a picture of the author along with a publicity blurb. The man had an interesting face—a commanding face, she thought to herself—and she liked the emphasis which the book seemed to place upon integrity and personal responsibility. "If you have troubles, you are the trouble," it said challengingly at one point. She became more and more intrigued. Then, glancing at her watch, she realized it was time to go. The young man at the counter rang the money through and slipped the books, with receipt, into a bag. She smiled at him. A whiff of her delicate perfume drifted across the counter. He gulped, adjusted his spectacles, smiled almost fiercely. "Thank you for coming in, ma'am," he said. He gazed at her with utter concentration and adoration as she turned and walked out of the door. The elderly, spinsterish lady who was waiting to be served coughed disapprovingly to gain his attention.

Chapter XIV

1958

He had made it all the way to the top. Now he was Premier Khrushchev, undisputed master of the Politburo and of Russia. He had topped his most powerful rival, Malenkov, and packed him off to be the director of a power station in a remote part of Kazakstan. Kaganovich, too, he had expelled from the Praesidium, charging him with having been Stalin's "chained cur and toady," and having "exaggerated his contribution to the development of transport and construction." He was now manager of a cement works in Sverdlovsk! He had also expelled the stuffed-shirt old Stalinist, Molotov, and sent him to the most obscure foreign service outpost of all, Ulan Bator. Historians would later take note of the fact, however, that they were not imprisoned, and they were not shot, as would have been the way during Stalin's regime.

A glass of black tea in his hand, Khrushchev sat at his mahogany desk, considering a manuscript which lay before him. But the tea had been only half drunk and was now almost cold. It was a gamble, of course, just as his move against the cult and terror of Stalin was still a gamble. But perhaps the small move that he was now contemplating would help the other, larger plan. He leafed again quickly through some of the pages of the manuscript, then stared for a few moments at the top page, on which were typed the words, "Sergeant Mihailovich," and below, "A novel by Grigori Antoniev." He had read the story and enjoyed it. It was earthy and honest. But the main thing was that it would help fuel his ongoing program of de-Stalinization. If these pages were to be published, not only within the confines of his own empire but in the West as well, it would rip the lid off his erstwhile master's brutal and inhumane treatment of millions upon millions of people—would bolster, and make all the more plausible and righteous his own bold initiative in denouncing the man who had ruled Russia in a grip of iron for 31 years. Nikita Khrushchev pushed the button of his intercom and said he was ready to see Nekrasov, his senior cultural advisor.

"This book by Antoniev that you gave me," he said after the man with the long, thoughtful face arrived. "What are we going to do about it? Any ideas?"

Gennadi Nekrasov hesitated. "The feeling of my committee," he began, but Khrushchev cut him short.

"I don't care about your committee," he said impatiently. "I am asking what you think, Gennadi. Should we allow it to be published or not?"

Nekrasov ran a finger around the inside of his collar. He was uncomfortable and it showed. However, he knew that one of the main reasons he found favour with this hard-driving, unpredictable man was that his judgments tended to be reliable even though they were not always orthodox. He was a man on a tightrope, he thought to himself. If he held back on his own personal opinion, or fudged it, he would be safe—but he might also be out of a job before long. He decided to speak truthfully.

"I may be biased, comrade Premier," he said, "but I like the book. I think it says some things which the people need to hear. I also think that publication at this time would enhance the policies which the Praesidium is pursuing under your leadership. At the same time, however . . ." Nekrasov paused.

"Yes? What is it, comrade?"

"I must point out to you that my committee is split down the middle. Three are in favour of allowing the book to be published, feeling that the advantages outweigh the disadvantages. The other three, however, are more cautious. They feel there is a danger in pushing your policy of de-Stalinization too far."

"Korelev is one of them, of course," said the bald-headed man moodily. "The chicken-livered toad always was afraid to stick his neck out."

"That is right. Korelev, Feoktisov and Yentutina were the ones voting against publication."

"But are you in favour? Do you think it could have positive results?"

Gennadi Nekrasov looked more thoughtful than ever. He felt his neck was stretching out further and further. But what the hell, he thought. This man Antoniev had had a hell of a time and come up with a good book. He deserved support. And if Russia was to come into greater freedom and enlightenment—which he, Gennadi Nekrasov, yearned for—then some people, somewhere, must take some chances.

"Yes," he said firmly. "I am in favour of publication."

Khrushchev smiled, his little, sharp eyes almost hidden in the paunchy folds of the lids.

"Good," he said. "Tell Ryumin that I will bring the matter up at the next session of the Praesidium." He clenched his beefy fist, brought it down with a bang on his desk. "We are going to light a fire under a few people, Gennadi," he said, chuckling. Nekrasov always found the Premier's humour infectious; he chuckled too.

"Yes," said Khrushchev. "I will make a personal recommendation in favour of publication. We will see what comrade Korelev says to that."

Nekrasov's thoughts strayed, for a moment, to his son, whose birthday was on the following day. Quickly, he brought himself back to the present. "Sorry, comrade. What did you say?"

"This man Andropovich," Khrushchev repeated. "How is he doing?"

"He is doing well."

"Any reservations?"

"Nothing serious. He is an independent person, and needs careful watching. But I find his ideas interesting and sound. It was he who brought Antoniev's book to my attention."

"By the way, I thought the first edition of *New Horizon* was excellent."

"I am glad that you are pleased, comrade Premier."

"How will the magazine handle Antoniev's book, if we go ahead?"

"I have talked with them about that. They will serialize it in three or possibly four editions. It should cause a sensation. Sales will be exponential."

"Very good." The Premier tapped his knuckles on the polished surface of his desk. "I would like to meet Andropovich. Antoniev too."

Nekrasov nodded. "If you wish, they could be invited to the dinner for cultural celebrities on September 25. You will be speaking there, you know."

"Very well. Nekrasov."

"Yes, comrade Premier?"

"My tea is cold. Ask Katerina to bring me some more."

People stamped their feet and arms to keep warm in the bitter cold. It was an hour before the bookshop was due to open, but a line of customers already stretched more than half a block. There were students; housewives; chattering office girls in smart, Western-style overcoats; businessmen and professional people in their forties and fifties; artists with shaggy hair and animated expressions, laughing and joking amongst themselves; even a sprinkling of elderly people braving the elements. They were all drawn together by the same compulsion—the desire to read a story called *Sergeant Mihailovich*, which was appearing in *New Horizon*. The story apparently had the backing of high officials in the Kremlin, even though it presented an unprecedented view of life in the prison camps and the abuses of the Stalin era.

The first printing of the magazine had sold out immediately. It was rumoured that a second printing would be available on this particular morning, hence the gathering of Muscovites determined to secure a copy. *Sergeant Mihailovich* was not only bringing excitement into the lives of thousands upon thousands of

Russians. It was also in the process of creating a literary storm whose effects would reverberate around the entire world.

* * *

The man with the direct, blue eyes and commanding presence stopped and looked at his watch. He had a few minutes to spare before his flight. He made his way to a bookshop and began browsing through some titles. He noticed that a display had been set up announcing a new book called *Sergeant Mihailovich*, by a Russian, Grigori Antoniev. "Lifts the lid off Stalin's Russia," said a blurb. "A searing exposé of life in a Siberian prison camp—strikes a blow for freedom everywhere," said another. "Incredible indictment of Stalinism, but also a triumphant affirmation of life," said a third. Dr. Lionel Denton picked up one of the books and studied it. There was a tender, thoughtful look on his face. He took the book over to the sales counter.

"I hope you enjoy it, sir," said the salesgirl, looking up at him with a hesitant smile. "We've been selling a lot of copies of this book."

Denton looked at the girl as she placed the book into a bag along with the receipt. He could sense that she was responsive to his presence. "I'm sure I shall," he said, returning her smile. "As a matter of fact I've been looking for it for some time. I hear it's a very exciting story."

The girl looked after him with interest as he moved away. Busy travellers passed through the shop by the hundreds, and one of her peeves about the job was that everything was so hurried and impersonal. All her customers thought about was that they had a plane to catch! This man had been different—friendly and calm. She didn't know why, but she felt uplifted.

Denton passed through customs and immigration and after a wait in the departure lounge, took his seat in the big blue and white Boeing airliner. He was on his way to England to attend a conference of cardiologists. It promised to be an important affair, and an opportunity to develop and nurture a number of useful connections. He had hoped to bring his wife, Elizabeth, but at the last minute it had seemed wiser for her to stay in New York. He wasn't worried about his clinic; he had a number of excellent doctors and specialists working with him who could be relied upon to handle things properly in his absence. What needed his wife's attention was his spiritual work, which was snowballing in volume and intensity. More and more people were beginning to wake up to the need for a shift in values. The old, traditional, materialistic approaches—even the old religious approaches—no longer seemed to satisfy. Since the publication of his book, *The Healing of the Nations*, which in a modest way had become something of a bestseller, he and Elizabeth had found quite a following gathering around them. For more than a year now they had been holding meetings and seminars in New York and elsewhere, discussing the principles put forward in the book.

Denton sat with Grigori Antoniev's book open on his lap, looking out of a window at the strawberry-coloured disk of the sun which was beginning to melt on the horizon. "Well done, Grigori," he said to himself. "Well done." He knew intuitively that with the emergence into more active and conscious expression of Antoniev—who, he suspected, might well be the physical clothing of the sun being, Pirius—the work for which he was responsible had taken an important step forward. It was a peculiar fact of his experience that while he knew there was a creative cycle at work, offering to mankind the opportunity to be healed and made new, he did *not* know the precise manner in which everything would work out. He knew, as it were, the destination, but not the route. "There's no road map, I'm afraid, Elizabeth," he had remarked to his wife on more than one occasion.

Sometimes, those who drew close to Denton, sensing his wisdom and authority, tried to get him to tell them what to do. They wanted him to take responsibility for their lives. This he utterly refused to do. "Take responsibility for your own life," he would say. It was the essence, in a way, of his teaching. He knew, better than anyone, the weight of responsibility that rested upon him to provide a trustworthy point of orientation and coordination for the emergence of the sun-design. But while he was willing to offer some guidance on occasion when it was really necessary, as soon as possible he impressed upon his followers the imperative need that they grow up and come into position themselves to perceive what they should do. Only in this way, he knew, could the creative process for which they were all responsible come into full and effective experience on earth.

Yet how reluctant human beings were, he had found, to do this. They would do anything rather than assume responsibility for themselves. They were always trying to put it off onto somebody else—their doctor, priest, government, guru, or whoever. Latterly, however, he had been delighted to see people coming forward who were finally willing to come clear of this fatal attitude of dependency. Take the Kents, for example. To be sure, they had not yet fully awakened to their true identity, but the process was definitely under way, and he had every faith in their persistence and integrity—characteristics vital, of course, for full awakening. He remembered with delight the initial letter he had received from Pamela. What a fresh, bright, eager spirit she had conveyed! William, a little on the cautious side, had not shown too much interest at first in Denton's premise that the problems of the world could never be solved by the same intellectually oriented approach that had created them, but only by the expression of a transcendent quality of spirit. He had, however, been willing to keep his scepticism in check while he proved out for himself whether what Denton said was true or not true. Lately, he and Pamela had been moving quickly into a position of real leadership in the embryonic body that was emerging under Denton's hand, and which was to be the means whereby people everywhere might emerge from the thick night of human ignorance and sense their place in the grand design of the universe.

Suddenly, the plane hit extreme turbulence. The voice of the captain, professionally calm and measured, came over the intercom, requesting the passengers to fasten their seat belts. The aircraft began bouncing up and down as if it were little more than a tiny Cessna. Denton became aware of a current of tension building rapidly around him. Here and there someone would laugh, or tell a joke, but he could sense fear close to the surface. The plane took a sudden, incredible lurch upward and the middle-aged man sitting next to Denton cried out in alarm. A stewardess walked by, checking seat belts, assuring the passengers that everything was all right, and nearly fell into Denton's lap.

Denton smiled reassuringly at the stewardess as she manoeuvred herself upright and continued along the aisle. Then he looked carefully at the man sitting next to him. He realized that this was not ordinary apprehension. The man was literally petrified. His face was white. He was staring straight ahead as if turned to stone. His hands gripped the armrests so tightly that the knuckles, too, were white.

Denton began to speak to the man in a gentle, matter-of-fact tone, telling him about the time when, as a young intern, he had delivered his first baby—in a taxicab. It was an amusing, indeed hilarious story, and had drawn many laughs over the years. It was hard to tell if the man was even listening, but he continued anyway, telling how finally, in the middle of crowded Manhattan, barely 300 yards from the hospital, he had successfully delivered a bouncing baby girl. As he finished the tale, two things happened.

The terrified man next to him gave a tiny, almost inaudible chuckle.

At the same time his hands slowly eased their grip on the armrests, so that colour began to return to his knuckles.

"You must have been pretty scared," he said, turning and looking at Denton and doing his best to muster a grin. "Just like I am now."

Denton laughed, a deep, infectious laugh that seemed to fill the whole plane.

"Yes," he said. "I was that all right."

"My name is Gates. John C. Gates." Almost sheepishly, the man held out his hand. Denton shook it warmly and introduced himself.

By the time the plane had cleared through the turbulence and things were normal, they were engaged in an animated conversation about hospitals, and what went on behind the scenes, with Gates eagerly asking him questions about his work as a cardiologist.

* * *

"Nurse? Where is the Kent baby, please?"

Kent looked through the long glass window into a room full of bassinets and babies.

The nurse smiled. "I'll bring him closer so that you can see him."

There he was, a tiny being. A pink blob of flesh with dark fuzz on the top of his head. Kent stared at the baby, entranced. He had never known a feeling like this before. That little bit of life on the other side of the partition had been born into the world because of him. Pamela too, of course . . . but without him it would not be lying there, for sure. He was a creator! He hurried up to the room where Pamela was resting. When she saw him, her eyes lit up. He took her outstretched arms and kissed her.

"It's happened," he said softly. "It's really happened. I looked at him through the window and I still can't believe it."

"Life is good," she said.

"He's so beautiful. I can't get over it. I've never been so all-fired excited in my life . . ." He looked at her and they both broke out laughing.

"I thought of some more names," she said. "What do you think of Jonathan Arthur?"

"Jonathan Arthur." He thought for a few moments. "I like the sound of it."

"Jonathan was a great friend and Arthur was a great king."

He kissed her again, at some length. "Darling!" She pretended to be shocked. "Have you missed me?" Her laugh was like a mountain stream.

Later, after returning home, he phoned Silas. It was getting late, and probably Silas had been getting ready to go to bed. He sounded irritable when he first picked up the phone. But that changed very quickly.

"Bill?" he said. "It's good to hear from you, boy."

"We've had a baby, Silas."

"What? I'll be damned. What is it?"

"It's a boy, Silas. He's a big fellow. Nearly eight pounds."

"I'm not surprised. How's Pamela?"

"She's very well, thanks."

"You give her my love. Congratulations, Bill. I hope I can see him one of these days."

"You certainly will. As soon as Pamela's back we'll have you over. I guess I'd better go. I've got more people to call. Take care of yourself and give my love to Violet."

The old man put the phone down. He felt warmed inside. It was a glow that made his nightcap almost unnecessary. He walked into the living room with such a big smile on his face that his older sister looked up in surprise.

* * *

Beresford sat in the sea lounge of the majestic Taj Mahal Hotel in Bombay, looking out over the harbour. His visit to India was almost over. He was due to catch the BOAC flight to London later that night. The deal with the Maharajah had worked out most satisfactorily from his bank's standpoint, but more than that—looking at things from a personal standpoint—his whole perspective on life had broadened dramatically. What had been impressed upon him, from the very moment he first set foot in the country, was the simple but vivid realization that there was a very much larger world out there than he and a lot of his friends and acquaintances in the West took into account. He felt an awakening sense of responsibility to be more inclusive in his thinking and in his perspective.

Until his arrival in Bombay ten days previously, he had never realized there could be so many people clustered together in such a small amount of space, with so many varied smells, and such an all-pervading feeling of busyness. Driving into Bombay from the airport, he had found himself almost unable to digest the incredible profusion of people and activities: old men and women patiently sweeping the dirty pavements; lorries, carts, motorcars, taxis and bicycles struggling for space with nimble pedestrians who seemed to escape certain death only by extraordinary acts of agility combined with a kind of telepathic sixth sense; shopkeepers and their relatives and friends gossiping together while keeping a sharp eye open for would-be customers; occasional cows with brightly painted horns; a policeman, here and there, directing traffic, doing his best to try to bring a little order into the situation; and pavement dwellers lying here, there and everywhere, on rags, bits of blanket, or the bare cement, and, of course, the inevitable beggars, sometimes mere children, holding up deformed limbs and asking him again and again, in soft, urgent voices, for aid.

It was a land of unbelievable contrast and diversity. He had glimpsed, passing through Bombay, the worst slums he could have imagined, and then been entertained by the Maharajah in a palace so luxurious and opulent that it made his own not inconsiderable estate in the Surrey countryside seem like a poorhouse.

Beresford caught the eye of a waiter and asked for another gin and tonic. As the man brought him his drink, he recalled some words that the Maharajah spoke as they watched one of his brothers passing down the street in his wedding procession, riding in all his finery on top of an incredibly bejewelled and flower-decked white horse. The Maharajah, a handsome man with a military moustache and a fine bearing, had said, "We kicked the English out all right, James, but frankly, we miss you a bit. Things haven't really been going all that well for us, you know."

The words had brought a tug to Beresford's heart. He had thought for a few moments, and then replied, a new vision already percolating in his consciousness, "I think we all need each other on this planet, Harinder."

Chapter XV

1960

Gennadi Nekrasov, senior cultural assistant to Premier Khrushchev, scratched his long nose, as he often did when he was thinking. The Minister's cocktail party was proving to be rather more lively than he had expected. There was the unmistakable smell of trouble. The party had opened with a dreadful outburst by the wife of a well-known musician. She had created a scene worthy of the attention of a Pushkin or Chekhov! The woman went into the bathroom to powder her nose and for some bizarre reason became incensed by the rows of French perfumes—Chanel, Lanvin, Schiaparelli—which lined the shelves. The guests in the drawing room of the old, high-ceilinged apartment were both horrified and intrigued to hear an extraordinary commotion. The musician's wife, well-known in Moscow for her outspoken views, was busy throwing Mrs. Zhukov's perfume bottles on the marble floor. At the same time she was swearing loudly and shouting such things as: "Disgusting hypocrisy!" "What was the Revolution all about, then?" "This is supposed to be a people's democracy!"

Not long after that affair was sorted out, Nekrasov was approached by Colonel Spassky and led to a quiet corner. Colonel Victor Spassky was a KGB officer whose department specialized in liaison with the Ministry of Culture and keeping an eye on cultural celebrities. He was a short, wiry man, cold and officious. More than that, thought Nekrasov, he was a boor with bad breath. Nekrasov had to concede, though, that he was extremely clever. More than once, Nekrasov had nearly lost his head because he underestimated Spassky's power and cleverness. He trod as warily and cautiously as a mountain climber crossing a crevasse whenever the man came near him.

"Good evening, Colonel, how nice to see you," he said warmly as Spassky came up to him. The KGB man merely gazed at him. Do you think I am some sort of insect? Nekrasov wondered. Finally Spassky spoke.

"I wish to discuss something with you, comrade," he said in a cold monotone. "It is concerning the writer Antoniev. You know that he wishes to go to America?"

"Of course. His new play is having its premiere there," said Nekrasov, his early warning system on full alert.

"Your department approved an exit permit, I believe?"

"That is so, Colonel. Antoniev's work has aroused considerable interest in the West and enhanced our image as a fair-minded society dedicated to the principles of coexistence and international understanding. We feel that allowing Antoniev to be present at the premiere of his newest play in Washington will exploit this. Who knows? It may also encourage those in the West who are sympathetic to our cause."

"Quite so. I have no quarrel with your decision, comrade. It is something else that I wish to discuss."

"I see." Nekrasov kept his voice and his manner neutral.

Colonel Spassky looked carefully around the room. "We want to bring some pressure on the writer Chuinovsky," he continued. "He has been becoming troublesome, as you know. We have arranged for a formal letter of censure of him and his work to be printed in *The Literary Gazette* in two weeks' time. We want Antoniev to be among those who endorse this letter. It will give the censure considerable clout. You see my thinking?"

He saw it. He did not like it. But that was beside the point, of course.

"Let me see," he said. "Are you thinking that Antoniev might refuse to sign such a letter? I think you are right. However if he knows that his American trip depends upon it he may be more cooperative . . ."

"Exactly, Nekrasov. The trip gives us the leverage we need." Spassky allowed himself a small smile. It scarcely made any impression upon the hard planes of his face.

Gennadi Nekrasov played with his nose some more. He nodded slowly. "It seems a logical ploy," he said. "It is just possible that it may work. It depends, of course, how important the visit is to Antoniev. However, it is the first time he has had an opportunity to go overseas. I would think he would give the matter serious consideration."

Spassky smiled again. "Excellent. Will you have someone speak to comrade Antoniev, or shall I?"

Nekrasov shook his head. "Don't worry, Colonel. I will speak with him. As a matter of fact he is coming to my office tomorrow."

"Excellent." Spassky paused reflectively. "Nekrasov?"

"Yes?"

"Please understand. We want Grigori Antoniev's name on the letter of censure. If this does not work we will have to think of something else."

"I see."

Arrogant, officious bastard, Nekrasov thought. These KGB men were all the same. They thought they could run all over everyone. They saw themselves as the bloody saviours of the country who could do no wrong. However he, Nekrasov, had an edge. He had the ear of Comrade Khrushchev. If this cockroach Spassky pushed him too far, he might drop a word in that ear and see what happened. Yes, he might do that; a man could take just so much. Nekrasov smiled warmly. He did not believe in giving anything away unless he had to.

"Have you seen Antoniev's new play?" he asked politely.

"No," the KGB man said shortly. He did not seem interested. Nekrasov doubted if he had ever been to a play in his life. He saw a chance of a little fun.

"It's brilliant. Quite brilliant," said Nekrasov, beginning to enjoy himself. "He analyzes the behavioural thought patterns of a small group of Czarist officials and shows how the basic human urge to procreate and be secure is balanced by a death wish having its roots deep in an unexplained phenomenon of the human psyche."

Spassky looked suddenly at his watch. "I must go," he said abruptly. "Excuse me, comrade." He retreated hastily. Nekrasov sighed with relief. He looked around for the pretty ballet star with whom he had been speaking earlier. Unfortunately, before he could spot her, his wife materialized and took firm hold of his arm, obviously determined not to let him out of her sight.

"Darling," he said, smiling at her.

Grigori walked alone beside a pond in Gorky Park. He stopped to look at a small flotilla of ducks moving, line astern, toward the shelter of the further shore.

Was it possible that Yevgeny Andropovich was wrong? His friend had been horrified at the suggestion that he endorse a censure of the writer Chuinovsky. Yet Grigori had a nagging worry that perhaps he did not see all the factors.

"Join a censure of Chuinovsky?" Andropovich had exclaimed as they sat drinking tea beside the samovar in his flat. "That would be quite unthinkable. No trip abroad could be worth it. If you were to join this censure—give it your support—it would not only increase the pressure on Chuinovsky, it would blight the hopes of hundreds of young intellectuals. No. You must not even think of it, Grigori."

His mother had been equally emphatic.

"It is too big a price," she said firmly as she put a plate of steaming rice pilaff before him. "What would your friends think of you? They would think you had betrayed them—and your own integrity. You will not do it, will you?"

He merely muttered vaguely when his mother pressed him. He had been noncommittal, too, when speaking with Andropovich.

For some reason that he could not explain, even to himself, he had a strong feeling that he needed to go to America. He sensed it had a purpose greater than he could presently envisage. At the same time the thought of publicly aligning himself with a censure of a gifted writer like Chuinovsky appalled him. He was, he thought ruefully to himself as he watched the ducks disappear into the reeds, on the sharp horns of a dilemma. He looked at his watch. It was time to go. He walked briskly toward the park exit. He had not resolved the dilemma, but there was one thing he did know. This was a decision which he must make on his own. The fact that Andropovich had been his teacher and his mentor could not be allowed to influence his judgment. The fact that his mother was telling him the same thing as Andropovich could not influence him either. He had to come to his own conclusion and take responsibility for it.

The crunch came three days later. Gennadi Nekrasov himself phoned and asked if he would meet him at the bathhouse. They went to the place on Sverdlovsk Street. It was a favourite venue for ministers, generals, top party officials and others with clout. Nekrasov insisted on paying, pulling the kopecks out of a neat leather pouch that he carried in his pocket. They draped themselves with the sheets which the grizzled attendant gave them, and holding their bundles of leafy birch twigs, made their way into the steam room.

"How's the steam today?" Nekrasov asked. A white-haired gentleman who sat perspiring on the very hottest balcony, six or seven steps up, nodded emphatically. "Excellent, comrade," he said. Every now and again he thrashed his rosy skin with his birch twigs.

"More water!" someone shouted authoritatively. Probably he was a field marshal, Grigori thought to himself. He fetched a tubful and threw it on the fire bricks in the oven. The steam rose up in a billowing, hissing cloud, as if answering a magician's summons. They found a place on a lower level and sat down. The steam room was so hot that it burned their nostrils. Here and there bathers thrashed themselves or others with their twigs. The room was filled with the particular ambience that men generate amongst themselves when they are relaxed and on their own. Grigori and Nekrasov chatted casually about this and that, joking with their neighbours, before finally fleeing into the relief of the change room. Nekrasov ordered two watery beers and they listened to a paunchy fellow—he was a senior supervisor at a defence plant—giving, to anyone who would listen, his ideas about how to handle women.

Wrapped loosely in their sheets, Nekrasov and Grigori made their way to an alcove.

"Well, my friend. You have a choice to make," Nekrasov said, his intelligent eyes watching Grigori closely. "I thought it would be better to work this out between ourselves than to let the KGB get into the act. What do you want to do? I must have your decision today if the exit permit is to be processed in time."

Grigori had still been undecided even when he woke up that morning. But he had told himself: "Don't worry. You will know what to do when the time comes. That is the way it has worked before. When you are with Nekrasov, you will know." Now, sure enough, he found that his mind was clear. He could not do it. Even though it would mean losing the opportunity to go to the United States, he could not do it. He could not support this attempt to destroy the reputation of a brilliant young writer. It would be a denial of his own integrity. It would betray everything he had lived for. It would betray the memory of his sergeant!

He looked at Nekrasov. Now that he had made his decision and let go of the trip to America he felt a hundred pounds lighter. "I would like nothing better than to go to America on this occasion, comrade Nekrasov," he said ruefully. "To see my play performed in the West would be immensely rewarding and stimulating. But I cannot do it. The price is too high. I cannot support an attempt to bully a young writer who believes in honesty and freedom. I must withdraw my request for an exit visa."

"I understand," said Nekrasov. He hesitated. Was there a hint of compassion on his face? "I will let you know if by any chance something can yet be worked out," he said quietly.

"You are very kind," Grigori said.

"It is nothing, Antoniev. You could not know this, but I read your writing avidly." Nekrasov smiled, showing several stainless steel fillings. "I particularly like Sergeant Mihailovich in your first book. In a few years, when my small son is older, I shall see that he too reads about him."

Grigori was embarrassed. He always felt that way when someone praised him. However he was also pleased. He respected this quiet, ironic man with his independent way of thinking and acting.

"May I say something even more personal?" Nekrasov probed the end of his long nose with a forefinger. "You are that rare thing, Grigori Antoniev, a person of integrity. Meeting you has added something to my life."

Nekrasov looked at Grigori apologetically. "I am sorry. I should not embarrass you in this way. Please forgive me."

Grigori gave a small laugh. "If you had seen me two years ago when I was drinking myself to death you would not say such things," he said softly.

"But I do say them," replied Nekrasov earnestly. "Even now you are calm—when most men would be angry or frustrated. Is it something you learned in the camps?"

Grigori's eyes seemed to look right through Nekrasov, focussing on some point far distant in time and place. "Perhaps," he said. "All I really know, comrade, is that there is a source within us which knows what we should do—and if we listen to that, things work out."

"That is how you survived Ust-Ulenov?"

"Yes. You could say that."

A short, tubby man broke into their conversation, shattering the sense of intimacy which had begun to develop.

"That was a good soccer game last night, eh, comrades?" the man said. When there was no immediate answer, he went on. "But what happened to Dynamo? Why did our team collapse like that?"

"It was all Chernenkov's fault," said Nekrasov, turning to him. "If he hadn't missed that pass from Sikorsky the game might have gone very differently. Sometimes a whole game rests on what happens in a certain critical moment."

Grigori nodded his head. "That is true," he said. "I have seen it myself. If Chernenkov had received that pass properly he would have got a goal and Dynamo might have won."

"You may be right, comrade," said the short man.

Nekrasov turned to Grigori, smiled, and gestured with his hands. "I am sorry," he said. "I must go. My desk is piled with papers."

They emerged onto Sverdlovsk Street from the bathhouse. "I will pass on your decision," said Nekrasov, eyeing Grigori intently. "Please. If you ever need help, feel free to give me a call. You have my number."

Gennadi Nekrasov walked off down the street towards his office, thinking hard. There was no question about it. When Spassky heard of Antoniev's refusal to endorse the censure against Chuinovsky the KGB man would become angry and dangerous. Undoubtedly, he would try to bring more muscle to bear in the situation.

Nekrasov had had quite enough of Spassky. If there was a way that he could cut the ill-mannered cockroach down to size and at the same time help Antoniev get to America he would be very pleased to do so. The whole business of trying to use blackmail on him had been unfair and improper from the beginning, Nekrasov thought. But if he was going to be effective he had better act now, before Spassky had a chance to manoeuvre. It would mean a personal word with Khrushchev. Khrushchev might feel a degree of sympathy for Antoniev. More to the point, he might share Nekrasov's view that the writer's proposed visit to America would affirm Russia's new cultural freedom. If so, things could still be turned around. It would only take a phone call from Khrushchev to the head men at the KGB, and Comrade Spassky would find himself out on a very shaky limb indeed. Nekrasov's thoughtful face broke into a relieved smile. He picked up his telephone and asked to be put through to the Premier's office.

It was the first time he had been in an airplane.

Grigori sat in a seat just behind the wing of the big Ilyushin. Members of the Robert Semeyusov Theatre Group laughed and chattered all around him, while a small squad of KGB men kept mainly to themselves.

He knew that this was his destiny, to be on this plane at this time, bound for America. The excitement and anticipation of it welled up within him. He laughed to think that it was because he had been willing to give up this trip to America rather than betray his friends, that it had not been necessary to lose the trip. He had seen the same principle proven out when he was in the camps. Those who were willing to do anything to stay alive—disregarding the voice of their own conscience—often ended up losing their lives. On the other hand, time after time he had seen that those who kept their self-respect and honour found their lives preserved. There was some sort of universal law involved, he believed.

Grigori sipped on the hot tea the stewardess had brought and he recalled how Nekrasov had phoned him at his apartment one evening as he was entertaining Chuinovsky and a group of other young writers. Wine had been flowing freely and the din was such that at first Grigori could not hear who was on the other end of the line. "Quiet. Please be quiet," he had said, holding one hand over the mouthpiece and gesturing furiously to everyone. As the hubbub died down he recognized Nekrasov's voice. At first he couldn't really believe what the voice was saying. He just stood there feeling as stunned as if a German tank shell had burst in front of him. When he put down the receiver, he stood silently for several moments. The room was completely quiet, everyone's face turned toward him.

"That was Gennadi Nekrasov," he said, almost back to his normal, laconic self. "I'll be going to America after all." He had grinned then, despite himself, a huge, happy grin that rolled years off his face, and impulsively put his arms around Mariya and gave her a big kiss. No sooner had he finished with her than Chuinovsky himself had flung his arms around him and kissed him soundly on both cheeks. The room exploded with excitement.

"I am so happy for you, Grigori," said Chuinovsky, his young face already streaked with tears. "It is good that there is some justice in this world. When you go to America, take the spirit of everyone in this room with you—friends, a toast to Grigori!" He had raised his glass, and spontaneously they had all stood to drink to him. Funny. That evening had been only a week ago and yet it seemed like ten years. Ten years since he had gone to his mother's place to give her the news and she had put her arms around him and pressed her face against his shoulder with silent emotion. After a long moment she had said to him, "You're like your father, Grigori. Your father always said that the most important thing was to be true to yourself."

The heavy-bosomed stewardess with the stern face came by and offered him a sandwich and some more tea. The plane stopped at Paris to refuel, then took off on its nonstop leg to New York. It was Saturday, July 3, 1960. Grigori's play, *The Adventures of*

Zelenaya, was due to be premiered in the United States the following Saturday at the National Theatre in Washington.

Stephanie Hampden, a pretty, green-eyed brunette on the staff of *The Washington Post*, looked unusually angry as she pounded away at the typewriter. From time to time she muttered furiously to herself. The man sitting at the next desk chuckled. "What's up?" he asked.

"How can people be so stupid?" she asked, looking up with a harrowed smile. "George Whittle, the House Appropriations chairman. Gosh, he makes me mad. He gave this slum clearance project a piddling $73,000, saying he needed more justification. It was spelled out in detail over a whole page, mind you. Then he turns around and recommends a one-line budget request for a new navy frigate without batting an eye!"

"That's the way it goes, Stephanie."

"Doesn't it make you angry though?"

"Sure it does. But what can you do?"

"I don't know. I sometimes think there must be something."

The phone on the man's desk buzzed. He picked it up and began talking. Stephanie Hampden typed three more paragraphs, then pulled the story out of the machine and checked it over. Her own phone rang.

"Hello," she said. "Stephanie Hampden here."

"I have a long distance call for you." It was the operator's voice. "Go ahead, please."

"Stephanie?"

It was James Beresford. Stephanie forgot all about Congressman Whittle and his committee.

"James. How good to hear your voice."

She had met the dark-haired, irrepressible Englishman two months before while covering the President's visit to London. Beresford was a member of the joint commission that handled trade relations between the two countries. His speech at a meeting attended by some of the President's top financial people as well as their English counterparts had been a welcome relief in a drowsy morning. Even though he had had to cover a great many facts and figures, his bright, lively spirit lifted the veil of boredom into which everyone had slipped. Afterwards she sought him out to ask some more questions, and he ended up inviting her out to dinner. They had had a thoroughly enjoyable time at the Dorchester and then he dropped her off at her hotel in a new blue Bentley that was polished as shiny as a guardsman's boots. It had been one of those unexpected times that can lift a reporter's spirits on a rather grinding and demanding assignment. He had not talked about his personal affairs but as a divorcée herself she thought she had been able to read the signs.

She heard him clear his throat at the other end of the line.

"I'm coming over to New York and Washington next week," he said. "I was wondering if we could get together?"

"I'd like that, James," she said, trying not to sound too excited. "When will you be in Washington?"

"I'm supposed to arrive on Wednesday afternoon at four o'clock. I'm taking a Pan Am flight."

"I could pick you up at the airport if you like."

"That would be terrific. I say, have you been working on any interesting stories, Stephanie?"

She laughed. "Not as many as I would like," she said. "But we keep trying. There's lots of competition in this town. Where will you be staying?"

"The Sheraton."

"James, I have an idea. Will you be here on Saturday of next week?"

"Yes, I will."

"I was wondering if you'd like to see a play with me? The office gave me two tickets to a premiere. It's called *The Adventures of Zelenaya.*

"Good heavens. What's that?"

"It's a comedy by the Russian, Grigori Antoniev."

"The man who wrote *Sergeant Mihailovich*?" He sounded excited. She smiled to herself. She appreciated his exuberance.

"That's right."

"Tremendous. I'd love to come with you. I enjoyed his book thoroughly."

"I understand he is coming over himself for the premiere. They're holding a reception for him at the Embassy afterwards.

We could go to that too if you like. I've got invitations."

"Sounds marvellous. I'll look forward to it. I'd better let you get back to work, Stephanie. I'll see you next Wednesday then."

"Good-bye, James. It's been good talking to you."

She replaced the receiver. For a moment, her eyes had a faraway look. Reynolds decided not to make the smart crack that had popped into his mind. Stephanie Hampden picked up her story and walked to the city editor's desk. She wondered what he would think about her treatment of Whittle.

"How can I thank you, Doctor? You have given me a new lease on life. I feel ten times better."

The Russian clasped Denton's hand warmly. He would have liked to give him a proper bear hug but was not sure whether it would be appropriate.

"I am glad I could be of assistance, Mr. Ambassador," said Denton as he walked Vladimir Volodya towards the door of his office. "I hope you will continue to improve." He paused, his eyes twinkling. "Please give my kind regards to your wife."

Volodya, who had served in his current post in Washington for three years, could not contain himself any longer. He put both arms round the American and kissed him soundly on the cheeks.

"You have been very good to me, Dr. Denton," he said. "I am glad that I insisted upon seeing you. Without your help I do not know . . . I do not know if I would still be here."

"I was very glad to do what I could, Mr. Volodya." Denton smiled warmheartedly as he opened the door for his visitor.

"By the way, I see that your distinguished writer, Grigori Antoniev, is coming to Washington in a few days' time," Denton added.

"Ah yes. You have read *Sergeant Mihailovich*, Doctor?"

"Indeed I have. A most unusual and fascinating book. I found it very moving. The tradition of great writers certainly continues in the Soviet Union."

Volodya smiled. "Yes," he said, "I think you're right. So you are probably aware that Antoniev's new play is to have its premiere in Washington shortly?"

"Yes indeed. I have already bought tickets. My wife and I will be bringing some friends—Congressman William Kent and his wife."

"Excellent. Excellent," said the ambassador. "If there is ever anything I can do for you, Doctor, please do let me know."

"You are very kind." Denton paused, hesitating.

"Yes, Doctor?"

"I was just thinking of something. I believe I read that a reception will be held for Mr. Antoniev after the premiere."

"That is correct. After the performance." The ambassador beamed. "Perhaps you and your wife and guests would like to attend? I would be delighted to arrange it."

Denton smiled broadly. "That would be a great pleasure," he said. "I would like to meet Mr. Antoniev very much. Thank you."

"Not at all. Not at all. I will see that you receive invitations."

Chapter XVI

1960

Inside the Soviet Embassy in Washington, lights burned brightly, glasses tinkled and a string ensemble played lilting Viennese waltzes. The occasional pop of a champagne cork mingled with the laughter and chatter as a prestigious slice of Washington society and an assortment of other guests gathered at a reception in honour of Grigori Antoniev and the Robert Semeyusov Theatre from Moscow. Earlier that evening, the troupe had given its first performance in the United States of *The Adventures of Zelenaya*, a comedy about a headstrong young poet of Czarist times.

"He doesn't say much, does he, the poor dear," giggled a well-known Washington hostess as she stared discreetly at the guest of honour. Grigori stood somewhat defensively beside a black marble bust of Lenin, surrounded by a group of inquisitive admirers.

"He's rather . . . rugged, isn't he?" the woman standing next to the famous hostess remarked thoughtfully. "A bit like a young bear."

"Would you like him to give you a bear hug, darling?" the

hostess asked with a naughty look. The other lady tittered softly; the thought intrigued her for a moment.

"Russians often are rather robust, aren't they?" she went on. "It's probably because of the kind of food they eat. All that bread and sausage. Do you think that's the reason, Harriet?"

But Harriet was looking elsewhere. "Look at that," she sniffed. "How dreadful. But Hetta Wyncoop never did have very much taste. What can you expect, really, from the nouveaux riches?"

A rather slightly built man of middle height with a whimsical expression on his face came by. He wore formal evening attire. Half a dozen or so medals decorated the front of his tuxedo. Ambassador Volodya had been commander of a squad which fought to the death in the streets of Stalingrad, only three of its members surviving.

"Good evening, Mrs. Weisbanger and Mrs. Liddell," he said, smiling. "How nice it is to see you. Thank you for coming this evening."

"Our pleasure, Mr. Ambassador," the ladies cooed.

"I do hope you are enjoying yourselves."

"Very much, thank you."

"Enjoy your drinks." The ambassador winked, motioned them closer. "But watch out for the vodka. It has an effect rather like a guillotine. One minute everything is fine, and then suddenly, pow!" He made a chopping motion with his hand. Grinning widely—he had several vodkas under his belt already—Ambassador Volodya moved on amongst his guests.

A waiter came by with a silver tray loaded with dark brown bread. Grigori helped himself generously. He had never been very relaxed in social settings and felt awkward in the glitter and sophistication of the gathering. Mikhail Barenkov, the good-looking young actor who had played the leading role in his play, saw him and came over.

"How's it going, comrade?" he asked cheerfully.

"Oh, all right, Mikhail. But I don't like this kind of party. It's too formal for my taste. How about you?"

"I cannot complain." Barenkov winked. "There are lots of attractive young ladies here. It's keeping me busy. Well, bear up, comrade. Only an hour or two to go. I hear you liked the performance."

"Yes indeed. The performance was excellent. You all did very well."

"There is always room for improvement," the actor said modestly. "But I think it came together all right. Tomorrow we will see what the critics say. But everyone I have spoken to thinks it will be a great success."

"You deserve it. You have all worked very hard."

"I was worried at one point. I was sure that the peasant girl was going to forget her lines."

"Mikhail?"

"Yes?"

Grigori had stiffened.

"Who are those two couples who have just come in? Do you know them?"

Barenkov glanced around and shook his head. "I have never seen them before," he said. "The fair-haired man is rather large, isn't he? And the woman with him . . . whew . . ." He whistled softly to himself. "There is someone I would like to meet. What a beautiful woman."

But Grigori was not listening. His senses had stilled. The same kind of thing was happening inside him that had happened long ago in the early months of the war when he awoke one morning with a strange sense of foreboding gnawing at his belly. Only now the foreboding was not of death but of something else. The middle-aged couple with the alive, commanding presence and the younger man and woman with them interested him. He wasn't entirely sure why but he felt attracted. There was something familiar about them. He felt an impulse to move in their direction, but a short, stolid-faced man stepped into his path, his face cracked in an unaccustomed smile. It was Zamratin, one of the KGB men.

"Good evening, comrade," said the policeman. He had a glass in his hand. Grigori guessed he had been imbibing freely, for his usually dour face was rosy and wore an almost blissful look.

"Good evening, Zamratin." The man stood teetering, trying to gather his thoughts. A furrow of concentration appeared on his forehead for a moment and then disappeared.

"I enjoyed your play. It was very funny. I laughed a lot." He hiccupped, then looked suddenly troubled. "Your glass is empty, comrade Antoniev," he exclaimed. "Let me fill it up. We must have a toast!"

The KGB man put a thick arm around his shoulders. "A toast," he said, in a voice even more gravelly and deep than Grigori's own. "Comrade Antoniev, let us drink to demon vodka."

"To demon vodka," said Grigori. They raised their glasses and clinked them; down went the vodka with a quick jerk of the head.

"And to your new play, comrade." They drank again. Three dutiful toasts later Grigori extricated himself and after two steps came face to face with the large, fair-haired man who had caught his eye earlier. At his side was the woman with the exotic figure and warm, generous face who had so impressed Barenkov.

"Mr. Antoniev?" The fair-haired man held out his hand. There was a friendly grin on his face. Grigori nodded. He was still puzzled by the feeling that he already knew these people. He reached out and shook the man's hand.

"Yes. I am Antoniev."

"My name is Kent. Congressman William Kent. This is my wife Pamela."

"We enjoyed your play so much," said the woman, shaking his hand also. "I found it very amusing. But it gave me lots to think about too. Is this your first visit to America, Mr. Antoniev?"

"Yes, it is." He was about to make a further remark when he realized the woman was staring at him intently with liquid brown eyes that contained a hint of puzzlement. "You must excuse me, Mr. Antoniev," said Pamela, "but it's almost as if I already know you. Isn't that strange?"

He was not expecting such a direct remark, or a question so much in tune with what was moving through his own mind. He reacted defensively.

"I don't know," he said. "I suppose it is." He felt awkward, ill at ease. He was tempted to make an excuse and move away but something would not let him do that. He made himself smile.

"I guess you find things very different over here," Kent said.

"Very different, yes. To be honest, I am rather confused."

The woman laughed, shaking her head of thick, black curls. Her laugh was a bright, happy sound and Grigori felt warmed by it.

"Those of us who live here get confused too," she said. "So don't let that worry you." She went on, serious now. "I read your book, *Sergeant Mihailovich.* It is outstanding, Mr. Antoniev. I don't know when I read a book which moved me so much."

"Thank you, Mrs. Kent. You are very kind."

"This Sergeant Mihailovich must have been a fine man. Were you good friends?"

There was a hint of pain in Grigori's eyes.

"Yes, we were."

"Your English is very good, by the way."

"You are kind. I have been studying it for a long time. It is not easy." He remembered something. "You came here with another couple," he said, glancing around.

"Yes. Dr. and Mrs. Lionel Denton. They are friends of ours." Kent had been watching Grigori closely. "He's a cardiologist. A very interesting man. You'd enjoy meeting him."

"He has his own clinic on Long Island, just outside New York," said Pamela. "He is an author too, by the way."

"There they are now," said Kent, catching sight of the Dentons across the room. "Would you like to meet them?"

Grigori hesitated, smiled almost shyly. "Yes, I would," he said.

"Come along then," said Pamela. She slipped an arm casually inside his and led him to a quiet corner. The Dentons were talking with a smartly dressed young woman and a man of about forty who looked like a successful businessman. They all turned.

"Lionel, I would like to introduce Mr. Grigori Antoniev," said Pamela. "Mr. Antoniev, this is Dr. Lionel Denton and his wife Elizabeth. As I mentioned, Dr. Denton is an author also. He has written a book called *The Healing of the Nations.* I hope you will read it some day."

A little awkwardly, Grigori clasped the doctor's long, artistic hand in his own rough one.

He looked into Denton's clear blue eyes.

There was the same sense of immediate friendship that he had known when he met the Kents.

"It is good to meet you, Mr. Antoniev," said Dr. Denton, his face lit by a peculiarly charming smile. "I have been waiting a long time for this pleasure."

"I am pleased to meet you," said Grigori, "and you, Mrs. Denton." He did not feel awkward anymore. He looked at the Dentons and the Kents and suddenly he wanted to laugh. He restrained himself.

"I am very happy to be here," he said. "Everyone is so kind."

There was a silence, not an awkward, empty silence, but a moment that was alive and bubbling, like champagne.

Dr. Denton spoke first: "May I make some more introductions? This is Miss Stephanie Hampden, a reporter for *The Washington Post*—so be careful what you say, Grigori—and James Beresford, from London, England. Miss Hampden, Mr. Beresford, this of course is Grigori Antoniev, and these are two special friends of mine, Congressman William Kent and his wife, Pamela."

They all shook hands. "I'm delighted to meet you, Mr. Antoniev," said the Englishman. There was a look of intense interest in his lively grey eyes. "Your play was superb. I enjoyed it thoroughly, just as I have enjoyed your books."

"I agree," said Elizabeth Denton, with her usual warm, radiant smile and emphatic way of speaking. "It was tremendous. I'm your biggest fan, Mr. Antoniev." Her love, as she looked at Grigori, was a potent, tangible force that he felt through his whole being.

"You really had the audience cracking up," said Kent.

"Cracking up?" Grigori asked uncertainly.

"He means everyone laughed a lot," said Pamela.

"Ah, I see." Grigori looked pleased. "That is good."

A waiter came by, elegant in a red and white uniform, bearing a tray of drinks. "Something new, ladies and gentlemen," he said. "This is called the Antoniev cocktail. Our barman has created it especially for this evening. Please take one if you wish."

"What's in it?" Stephanie asked, curious.

The waiter looked mysterious. "I am sorry. I am not supposed to say," he said conspiratorially, pretending to look over his shoulder.

"Nothing too lethal, I hope," said Beresford, taking a glass.

Stephanie Hampden looked at Grigori. "May I ask you something?" she said. "All those years that you spent in the prison camps. How did you manage to survive?"

They all waited with interest for the answer. A small smile crossed his lips.

"Sometimes I wonder myself," he said. He stopped smiling. The expression on his face became hard and remote. "Many men who were stronger than me did not. They died of illness, or were shot. Some became animals, fighting and killing each other over a crust. Others became like walking dead, caring little about anything. I think that was the saddest fate of all. But to answer your question, I believe it was because I had a feeling of purpose."

"What sort of purpose?" Stephanie Hampden pressed home her questioning.

"I realized there was something I had to do in my life, and that was what kept me going."

"Are you talking about the book that you wrote?"

"Yes."

"It gave you something to live for?"

"Yes."

"What about Sergeant Mihailovich? He must have been a big influence on you."

"He was, yes." Grigori's face softened. "He was a great man. I thought the world should know him."

"Was that what started you on the book?"

"Yes."

"What about Valeri Konstantin, the camp philosopher?"

"That is not his real name, but he was a very special friend too. Many times when I was confused or angry he would sit down and talk with me. That is something that is difficult to understand if you have not been inside the camps, Miss Hampden. Friendships are deeper than on the outside. And although there is suffering, there are times of supreme happiness also."

Grigori stopped. "Please, do go on," the reporter said, writing briskly in a small notebook which had materialized out of her handbag. "This is all most interesting."

Grigori frowned. His jaw set in an obstinate line. "Please," he said. "You must excuse me. I have spoken too much about myself."

"Thank you for what you have shared with us," said Pamela gently.

A member of the Embassy staff came hurrying towards them.

"Miss Hampden?" he enquired. "There is a telephone call for you. Would you come this way, please?" Stephanie Hampden grimaced, but followed the man across the room and down a hallway.

Dr. Lionel Denton looked thoughtfully at Grigori, Beresford and the Kents. "How interesting that we come from such varied countries and backgrounds, even from as far as Russia," he said. His voice, though quiet, had a compelling quality to it. Each one followed his words intently. "Yet I have always felt," Denton continued, "that there is a place where people may meet and be true friends, regardless of their differences."

"I assume you're not talking about a church or a synagogue?" There was a suspicion of a grin on Beresford's face.

"No, not a physical meeting place," said Denton, seriously. "A place within oneself where true qualities of character may grow. Uprightness, shall we say, and understanding, a willingness to give."

"Delicate things, Doctor," said Kent.

"Very delicate," he agreed. "Yet how important it is to awaken to such qualities and express them. This is how we discover our true selves."

Denton had chosen his words very deliberately. He was of course keenly aware of the unique opportunity afforded him during these few moments. The compulsions of life—often dismissed by human beings as mere coincidence—had brought together these four people who had a very particular part to play with him in the work for which he was responsible. He was also aware, however, of the need for caution. Although a considerable degree of blending had already occurred between the four sun beings and their human clothing, and he knew that Magnabaran, Pirius, Haldan and Mirana were actively listening to him, Prince Tauhelion knew too that he could not speak freely yet.

Pamela had been nodding her head as he spoke. "I agree with you entirely," she said, "and even the very future of our planet may depend on such awakening."

Denton had a feeling that within a few moments they would be interrupted. He thought quickly as to what would be the most useful thing to say. This apparently coincidental gathering in fact marked the beginning of an important new cycle, and he longed for them all to recognize each other as a team.

"Exactly," he said, smiling at Pamela, "and I would say that in waking up we recognize close connections with others who are moving on the same wavelength." He allowed his eyes to rest for a brief, penetrating moment on each one. He relished the strong current of feeling building among them. He decided to take one more step. "People always tend to think that someone else will take responsibility for what needs to be done," he said. "But just suppose you are the ones—with others, of course—who will restore this planet to order and to beauty?"

Pamela's heart was pounding. She slid her hand into Kent's, and he gripped it with surprising force. "I can only speak for myself," he said. "But I feel each of you is a close friend, even though we may have just met. It seems inevitable that we should continue as friends and stay in contact."

Beresford threw back his head and laughed. "Isn't this amazing?" he said. "Here we are, in the middle of an Embassy party, feeling like long-lost kin, certain that we have something crucial to do together!"

"Yes," said Grigori, his eyes glowing with understanding and relief. Somehow all he had gone through now began to make sense.

"Here we are together indeed," Prince Tauhelion thought to himself, "a new stage set." Out of the corner of his eye, he saw Stephanie returning. "I look forward to being in touch with all of you and seeing what will unfold," said Denton, glancing affectionately around the circle. "My wife and I travel frequently, but when we are home we would love to have you call or visit us anytime, and of course you can always write to me at my clinic. By the way, Grigori," he added, "I expect to visit the Soviet Union within a few months to attend a conference. We may have an opportunity to meet again then."

Stephanie approached, looking slightly dismayed, and took Beresford's arm. "Could you take me home? I'm so sorry to have to leave all of you, but there's an emergency."

"Yes, of course," he replied.

"I do hope we will meet again," Stephanie said, arrested for a moment by the substance she felt among them.

Beresford felt an unfamiliar pang as he said his farewells and left the still pool of communion, suddenly surrounded again by the brittle chatter of the reception.

After their departure, Grigori's gaze was riveted again on Dr. Denton. His heart had leapt at the thought that this man, who had somehow stirred a longing—for his own father?—would be in his homeland. "Please. Tell me where your conference is and when you would have time free," he said. "I will be there."

Those remaining were drawn again into the reception swirl. A few moments later Lionel and Elizabeth Denton walked out onto the balcony. A fresh wind had sprung up. They looked above the lights of the city to where the constant stars moved in intricate harmony. A wave of thanksgiving and relief moved through Prince Tauhelion as he thought of the four precious beings who were moving into position to serve consciously with him and his consort. They would—he was sure—open the door for many more.

Chapter XVII

1962

The two men set out along the narrow, lonely beach, walking only a few feet from the water's edge. They were deep in thought. Every now and again they stopped, sometimes facing one another, sometimes looking out over the ocean. From a distance, they looked like any other beach-walkers. Both wore deck shoes and casual pants. Only if you had come closer would you have seen the presidential seal of the United States emblazoned on the leather jacket which one of the men wore. At that point you would also have noticed the small group of men who trailed at a discreet distance behind the two. Their task was the protection—night and day—of the man who wore the leather jacket.

They had slipped quietly out of Andrews Air Force base that morning, and landed discreetly by helicopter on a nearby golf course. It was fitting to the occasion, Kent thought to himself, that the sea off Hyannis beach was grey, and a storm was brewing. For was there not a storm of far vaster proportion brewing upon the world scene, affecting the lives of every single one of the earth's inhabitants? As they walked along the ocean's edge, Kent was aware of the enormity of the responsibility which rested upon his companion. President John F. Kennedy was still youthful and good-looking, but the strain of his office—and the current crisis over Cuba—was clearly to be seen on his face. At the same time, Kent was keenly aware that he, too, had a responsibility of a very specific kind now. He had been involved ever since the President's phone call the previous day, asking if he would be available for a private meeting at Hyannis Port, and hinting that it had to do with a crisis over Cuba.

The Kennedys and Kents had been friends—up to a point—for more than two generations. Jack and William, particularly, had always got on well. They had been friends at school, and a deeper friendship and trust had developed since Kent's entry into Congress. Nonetheless, the request to meet the President at Hyannis Port had come as a complete surprise. He had made arrangements immediately, of course, to comply with the invitation. The mid-term congressional election was only two weeks away, and he had had to cancel two vital speaking engagements, pleading a cold and fever. The tone of the President's voice, however, had left no doubt that a matter of the utmost importance was involved.

The smell of the wet sand and seaweed was pungent and good. The man in the leather jacket stopped a moment, extracted a cigar from his pocket and lit it. The scent mingled with the scent of the ocean as they walked on. Kent thought he had never seen Kennedy in an angrier mood. Yet even as they walked, he began to relax and calm down.

"I usually come here alone," the President said, puffing on his cigar, "when I've got to put my neck on the line and the shit is bouncing off the fan. But for some reason, Bill, I wanted you along this time. I don't know how much you've heard. God knows we've tried to keep everything under wraps. But we've got a full-scale emergency on our hands. Khrushchev is lying through his teeth, the son of a bitch. He keeps insisting there are no missiles on Cuba, but we have pictures to prove it. And they're not just defensive missiles. There are goddam offensive missiles being deployed in Cuba that could hit Washington. The question is what the hell are we going to do about it? The military want to go in and bomb the shit out of the island or launch an invasion, and they've got Acheson and Fulbright on their side. But how safe is an air strike? If we missed just one missile, maybe that missile could wipe out Washington. And what about the Russians who would be killed? I don't like it, Bill. It's too drastic. Too dangerous. Khrushchev's an unpredictable man. I want to give him as much chance as I can to retreat gracefully."

They stopped and looked seaward to where a small sloop was battling its way through the grey seas. Every now and again its mainsail almost disappeared from view as it heeled to the stiff breeze.

Kennedy pushed his thick mop of hair back from his face and gave a tight grin. "Lucky guy," he said. "All he has to worry about is when to take in another reef. He hasn't a clue tomorrow could be doomsday."

They walked on in silence for a few minutes. "My own feeling is for a blockade," the President said abruptly, turning and facing Kent. "Bobby feels the same way. We've got to do something. Adlai wants to negotiate—offer to take our missiles out of Turkey and quit Guantanamo—but I told him it would be taken as weakness. The feeling I got from Khrushchev in Vienna is that he's going to keep on pushing until he runs into something that he can't push anymore. If we back down on this one Berlin will be next."

Kennedy put a hand to his face and rubbed his chin. His eyes, as he looked at Kent, were tired and filled with pain, so that they seemed almost grey. He opened and closed his fist two or three times, unconsciously seeking to release the tension he was feeling.

Kent was impressed again, as he had been before on occasions, with the awful loneliness of the President. Suddenly, he knew why he had been summoned to this remote stretch of beach, to this unsung meeting. It was to be a friend: to share, if he could, something of the burden that pressed down upon the other man. Kent remembered the verdict of people like former Secretary of State Dean Acheson on Kennedy's performance at the 1961 Vienna summit. Acheson felt that Khrushchev found Kennedy weak and vacillating; a pushover because he had not followed through decisively at the Bay of Pigs and taken Cuba. Of course, that tended to be Acheson's own view of Kennedy. He had once told Kent, as they rode down a Senate elevator together, that Kennedy was not a great man; did not have the stature to make a president. Kent had not agreed with that assessment. "Perhaps he just hasn't had a chance to show his greatness yet," he had murmured.

Well, one thing was sure. The current crisis would test the President to the ultimate. But it would also, Kent reflected somberly, test America and Russia to the ultimate. Would there be common sense, along with courage? Would there be the essential ability to bend, when humility was required, or be strong and unyielding, if that really was necessary? Or would mankind simply annihilate itself because of pigheaded obedience to outworn concepts of national honour and patriotism?

He was aware of a tremendous sense of stability and calm flooding his consciousness and moving through him. He sensed that the President was looking to him not just for support, but for direction and understanding. He had an almost eerie feeling that what he said in the next few seconds, as the two of them trod the little ridges of sand which the tide had recently left behind, was vital to the destiny of mankind.

Denton's words of the previous evening came vividly to his mind. He had phoned Lionel to let him know he would be meeting the President at the latter's request, and that it concerned a crisis over Cuba. "An invisible influence of sanity and common sense is being extended all the time by those who are true to the truth of their own being," Denton had said. "But we do have the responsibility also of letting that invisible influence find tangible form in words when it is appropriate and possible. I am delighted that you have this opportunity to speak directly with the President—I am sure it will be a significant factor in the right handling of this situation."

Kent addressed the President. "I agree with you, Jack," he said. "Technically, I suppose, a blockade is an act of war, but it seems to me that it is far and away your best option. I think you are right when you say that words mean nothing to Khrushchev. You have to show in a concrete way that you mean business—like you did when you ordered those tanks to move through the Russian sector into West Berlin. My feeling is that a blockade will accomplish this, but give you the flexibility to get tougher if you have to. I think drastic military action is unwise and could very well precipitate war, but doing nothing would be folly also. As I see it, a blockade is the least you can do, and also the most you should do—a balanced response to the situation."

The President stopped, and looked out to sea again. "Thank you, Bill," he said. He smiled ruefully. "But there's one hell of a lot of pressure on me to let the military have their way. You've no idea." His head and shoulders slumped a little.

Kent wished he could simply speak to the President of the truth; tell him straight and plain that he was not just a poor, isolated human, struggling under this great burden, but an incarnate being whose true identity was eternal.

But of course he couldn't do that.

The President would think he was nuts.

So he said as much as he could say. "If a blockade is the right thing, it will prove itself out," he said, with a smile.

Kennedy pulled himself upright again. He looked up for a moment at the sky, where menacing grey clouds were passing by in formation.

"You're right, Bill," he said. "That's all that really matters, isn't it? Just that we do the right thing. You know something? It's the children. If it weren't for the children, it would be so easy to push the button. But just think of the millions of children all over the world whose fate is in my hands. I can't condemn them to suffer and die because of a mistake that I make."

A lone seagull came swooping down near them, casting a beady eye in their direction just in case they were handing out any food.

They made their way back to the Kennedy compound. The country's top military men arrived a few hours later. They had come to present the President with their recommendation: it was for an air strike.

At all costs, the President of the United States thought to himself, he must keep his composure. It would be all too easy, in the face of this crisis, to make a hasty—and therefore, probably disastrous—move. Somehow, the twenty-five minutes that he had spent with Bill Kent on the beach had helped bring a new sense of stability—renewed his courage. Not only that though. Something had clarified in his mind. He knew now that his earlier hunch was correct. This crisis demanded a balanced approach, neither too much reaction nor too little. But while the necessary preparations continued, it was imperative to maintain the cloak of secrecy which he had insisted upon ever since the crisis began. Holy Jesus, he thought to himself, how long ago was that? How long ago since Bundy had walked into his bedroom in the White House at 6:30 in the morning to tell him they had confirmed photographic evidence of missiles on Cuba? It seemed like five years, but he knew it was only five days . . .

The President looked up from his desk and stared broodingly at the familiar painting hanging over the mantel of his office. It showed the American ship Bonhomme Richard engaging the British Serapis. With the mid-term election so close, he thought to himself, he had no choice but to continue his campaigning schedule. Cancellation—on almost any pretext—would arouse immediate suspicion and speculation. It was a miracle that the cat was not out of the bag yet. God, the antics they had got up to. Since a large collection of limousines would have been a dead giveaway, his crisis advisers often went first to the Treasury Building, making their way from there to the White House by means of a secret underground passage. On one memorable occasion, ten top officials of the United States had piled into a single car to ride from the State Department to the crisis centre in the White House basement. Because of the need to maintain normal routines and schedules, crisis meetings had often taken place at midnight. Fortunately, the White House press corps was in total disarray because of the political campaign. Every journalistic antenna was pointed in that direction. None of the reporters could spare time or energy to consider the larger world scene.

Playing out the extraordinary drama every step of the way, the President left Washington Friday, October 19, on his campaign weekend. In Cleveland hundreds of thousands of unsuspecting people lined the motorcade route from the airport to Public Square in the heart of the city. "These are the issues of the campaign," he shouted. "Housing, jobs, the kind of tax program we write in the coming session, the kind of assistance we provide for education . . ." He spoke with fervor and conviction. Anything to keep people's minds away from Cuba . . . reporters' minds away from Cuba . . . In the Springfield State Fair Grounds livestock pavilion, he told the farmers what they wanted to hear. "In the last twenty-one months we have not, by any means, solved the farm problem, but we have achieved the best two-year advance in farm income of any two years since the Depression," he said.

It was playacting, of course. While, physically speaking, he was in solid, well-grained mid-America, his mind was thinking of Cuba. More and more, he was sure that the worst course of all would be to do nothing. A blockade would, God willing, make possible a resolution of this crisis without resort to the unthinkable. Did Khrushchev think he was too young, too immature, too indecisive or inexperienced? Did he think he could push him around, win points at his expense? Khrushchev had another think coming. A young woman pressed toward him out of the crowd with a garland of flowers in her hands. He grinned, pushed through his security men, gave her a kiss she would remember for the rest of her life. Summoned back to Washington for further urgent consultation on the crisis, he told his brother Bobby and his advisers, "It's going to be a blockade."

He announced the blockade—it was called a "quarantine"—in an address to the American people at seven p.m. Monday, October 22. For the first time, he told how there were nuclear missiles in Cuba capable of destroying Washington, D.C., or other cities. He called Khrushchev's action a "deliberately provocative and unjustified change in the status quo which cannot be accepted by this country if our courage and our commitments are ever to be trusted again by either friend or foe." He added that any missile launched from Cuba would require a "full retaliatory response upon the Soviet Union." As Soviet merchant ships and submarines drew inexorably closer to the picket line of American ships that waited for them 500 miles from Cuba, the crisis moved to a flash point. The U.S. commanders had been ordered to stop the first ship with a cargo hold deep enough to carry a missile. What would the Russians do when one of their ships was intercepted?

* * *

Shock and disbelief was followed quickly by anger and fear as he digested the news that the Americans were going to blockade Cuba. The announcement had been conveyed to him through official channels from Washington just an hour or so before Kennedy's address to the American people.

Kennedy had called his bluff. The man whom he had judged to be immature and indecisive—young enough, after all, to be his son—had proved to have more mettle than he thought. He had met steel with steel. It had seemed such a brilliant move; such a daring initiative. In one masterful stroke he would have ensured Cuba's safety—the Americans would never dare to invade if it meant the risk of a nuclear strike on their own mainland—and also tilted the whole balance of power in his favour. With the missiles in position and targetted on American cities, he could have walked into the United Nations General Assembly and casually revealed his nation's strategic superiority. And he had planned to do just that.

Now the plan was in serious jeopardy—for it had hinged on their being able to install the missiles without U.S. detection.

Not only was it in jeopardy. It looked very much as if it might backfire. Instead of him teaching Kennedy a lesson, as he had anticipated, it could be that he was going to be taught a lesson.

As the days passed and the crisis reached increasingly acute proportions, the master of Russia knew that he had to make a momentous decision affecting the future of the entire planet. It would also, he knew very well, affect his own personal future. There had been mumblings and rumblings of disaffection in various quarters. His agricultural policies had come under fire—and his rift with China. To back down over Cuba would be seen not only as weakness, but as failure. It was the old story. Succeed in some desperate, daring venture and the people loved you. Fail, and they wanted your head on a platter. In this instance there was no question that China, and his other enemies, would use any retreat on his part as an excuse to castigate and condemn him. But what was the alternative? There was only one alternative. A confrontation which would end, almost inevitably, in the horror of thermonuclear war.

Premier Nikita Khrushchev had seen many horrors in his day. He had had more than a little notion of what Stalin was up to in those terrible years before the Great Patriotic War. Had he not shared, on occasion, in the dirty work, justifying it to himself on the grounds that it was necessary to bring Russia into the twentieth century?

But what horror could compare with the horror of a nuclear war that would leave the earth a charred, blackened ruin in which neither people nor creatures could live?

In the strange, contradictory mix of his character, the spark of humanity which had always been present, nurtured by his faithful wife, Nina, made its way to the surface.

He could not condemn mankind to destruction.

There was, he knew, only one reasonable decision. He must order the ships bearing missiles and bombers to Cuba to turn back, regardless of whether he himself would lose face, or his country would lose face. With luck, it would not be a total loss. If he could obtain an unconditional assurance from President Kennedy that he would not invade Cuba, this could even be touted as a victory—a major foreign policy achievement.

Over the objections of many of his generals, he prepared a message to be transmitted to the U.S. State Department. It was a plea for peace. Though it was not stated specifically, the letter offered to withdraw the offensive weapons under UN supervision in return for an end to the blockade and assurances that Cuba would not be invaded.

It was not quite the end of the crisis. There were a few more surprises; a few more moments of agonizing suspense. But at nine o'clock on Sunday morning, October 28, a special radio bulletin from Moscow announced in clear, categorical terms that Premier Khrushchev had ordered that work on the missile sites be halted, and the missiles crated and returned to Russia. He lived up to his word. The forty-two missiles were taken down and shipped home while the U.S. navy counted them. The sites were destroyed and the bombers recrated and sent back to Russia.

Chapter XVIII

Through the immensity of space and the eternity of time the solar system moves in sublime order and harmony, yielding naturally and easily to the cosmic rhythms and compulsions that guide entire galaxies and systems of galaxies on their courses, accomplishing, moment by moment, the purposes inherent in those rhythms and compulsions.

As the solar system participates in this cycle of movement, it meets, and for a moment of cosmic time blends with, a huge galactic cloud that is itself being moved by those same rhythms.

As the sun and its planets, including the earth, move closer into the heart of this passing cloud, changes occur in the nature and density of the electromagnetic fields in which the solar system is enveloped.

These changes have effect in various ways. Amongst other things, they directly affect the creation that has been brought into form on the surface of the earth; particularly, that called man.

For eons of time up to this point, men and women have lived in perfect harmony with the cosmic pulsations and laws governing the universe. Self-centeredness is unknown. Disease and suffering are unknown. Fear and conflict are unknown. There is simply a state of nobility; an awareness of oneness; a sense of belonging in the overall scheme of things.

With the coming of this invisible galactic cloud, it is recognized that special care will be necessary insofar as the function of humankind is concerned. This is because the cloud will act as a "veil" which for a short period of time—20,000 years or so by the human calendar—will very slightly modify the creative field enfolding the earth.

A warning is given, therefore, by those in positions of authority, to be careful.

Unfortunately, one or two forget . . .

They allow deviation to occur. Oh, such a small deviation, to begin with. So tiny, so innocent, seemingly. A very tiny substitution of personal desire and opinion in place of the perfect compulsion and perfect design already present and operative.

It couldn't possibly do any harm, they thought.

But, of course, it did. And as more and more people began to experiment with the same self-centred way of thinking and acting, ignoring the truth which was present, but which by its very nature could not be imposed, the results grew more and more destructive, until finally we have the situation as it exists on earth today . . .

But the rhythms of the cosmos move on. The purpose of the cosmos moves on.

The solar system begins to move clear of the galactic cloud within which it has been veiled, with the result that the creative electromagnetic field enveloping the earth begins to intensify.

It is not by chance that in the short space of fifty or a hundred years, mankind has learned to fly, has set foot upon the moon and pioneered the age of electronics, has become involved in two world wars and developed weapons unprecedented in their destructive ability . . .

The fire of cosmic radiation permeating and enfolding the solar system, the earth, and the bodies, minds and hearts of human beings, is increasing in intensity, just as the sun increases in intensity when it comes clear of cloud.

Man cannot help but react to the intensity . . .

Lord Perakleos was, quite rightly, more than a little proud of his observatory. He had personally designed and created the various instruments with which it was equipped. These included a unique starscope which, when properly focused and tuned, allowed him not only to observe various stars and planets, but also to listen to the different patterns of music that emanated from each one.

Now, however, Lord Perakleos was not listening to music, however heavenly. He was studying another screen which kept him informed of happenings on earth. From the serious, almost sombre cast of his countenance, it was evident that he was considering a matter of grave import.

"They have avoided self-destruction by a hairbreadth," he pronounced, turning to Lord Diaxos and his other guests. "This Cuban missile crisis is the closest that the human race has come to complete and utter annihilation since the time of Noah."

Diaxos came over, accompanied by the two envoys from Rigel, Gordhan and Lamar.

"By a hairbreadth is correct," said Diaxos, studying the screen. "Obviously the focus provided by Prince Tauhelion has been taking effect. There was *just* enough stability and integrity and common sense available to avert disaster."

"Yes," said Perakleos, nodding his head. "It is interesting that Tauhelion's four primary points of agreement at this time all came into conscious position to serve with him shortly before this crisis—in 1960, if I remember correctly. If Tauhelion had not had these four with him, along, of course, with many, many more the world around who are also beginning to awaken to the real extent of their spiritual responsibility, no doubt the earth would already be in ashes."

Lamar spoke. "How long can mankind teeter thus on the edge of annihilation?"

Perakleos moved over to an elaborate console which ran along the full length of one wall. He pushed some buttons and presently the console lit up with a variety of colours. A soft, melodious hum filled the room.

"How long have they got?" he said softly. "I can tell you in a few moments, Lamar."

The hum ebbed and flowed in intensity. A series of figures and other symbols flashed on a circular, purple-tinted screen.

"Let's see," said Perakleos, as he studied the figures and busied himself with some calculations.

"It is now October 1963, as time is measured on earth. Considering the intensity of the electromagnetic pulsations already permeating and enveloping the earth and its inhabitants, and the even greater intensity which will be known in the very near future, I would say that they have something on the order of twenty or thirty years, at best, in which to change their approach and accept the way things really work in the universe. That, of course, would be the easy way. The fire of cosmic love would then simply burn up the dross that is present in human minds and hearts. There would come release from the awful tyranny of fear, jealousy and hate. The alternative, I suppose, is a thermonuclear war of man's own making, which would also get rid of the dross, but at what a price . . . it would write finish to the creative work with which we have been concerned on earth . . . we would have to begin all over again . . ."

Lord Diaxos, normally outspoken to the point of being brusque, was strangely tender.

"The time of the end," he said quietly, "when a final choice must be made on earth between life or death, love or hate, the way of integration or disintegration. How many will resist the compulsion to change, condemning themselves thereby to oblivion, and how many will rise up in their integrity and welcome that necessity, coming into the increasing experience of true freedom and ease?"

"The experience that once was natural for all mankind," Perakleos added.

A look of utter puzzlement and amazement was on the faces of the two envoys.

But why would mankind choose disintegration and death?" they asked, speaking almost simultaneously.

Diaxos and Perakleos sighed, shaking their heads. "That, my dear friends," Perakleos replied, "is a mystery—a mystery which will never be solved. There is no rational explanation for man's insane behaviour; for his refusal to accept and harmonize with the creative pulsations which bring forth order and beauty everywhere we might look in the glorious cosmos, except, alas, this little speck of dust we call Earth."

There was a silence for a while in Perakleos' observatory. Then Lamar spoke again.

"I don't wish to seem overly curious," he said. "But what are some of the things that you see as likely to occur during this next critical time on earth?"

Perakleos was thoughtful. His eyes seemed to be gazing off into some far reach of space.

"There will obviously be more and more upheaval," he said quietly. "For example, the social revolt by young people will increase and spread as they attempt to pioneer a new culture to replace the traditional values of mainstream society. It will not yet be the genuine article, of course, but it will be a step, possibly, in the right direction. There will be other steps, too—an awakening, for instance, to the awful devastation and pollution that mankind has been inflicting upon the earth. At the same time we will no doubt see an increase of terrorism and conflict everywhere as people become more and more desperate in their efforts to defend some ideology or belief, or impose it on others. I would not be surprised if there will even be those who will fight for peace, a strange state of affairs if ever there was one . . ."

Hestus, consort of Diaxos, interjected, "I have a feeling that women will be in revolt too, objecting to what they perceive as rigid and unfair attitudes on the part of men."

"Very likely," Perakleos agreed, smiling. "Well, perhaps the men need to be shaken up a bit . . ." He paused, seeking the right words. "There has been so much honour, integrity and dedication shown by so many members of the human race over the centuries," he went on, "maintaining a thread of greatness and hope. It is unthinkable that this will all go for nothing. A portion of mankind, I am sure, will rise to the challenge and accept the responsibility which must be accepted while there is still time. Through this portion, however large or small it may be, the transformation of consciousness that is essential will occur." The radiance of Perakleos' spirit filled the room with a golden glow as he looked around him. "All of this, however, will be another story."

ABOUT THE AUTHOR

Born in England, Chris Foster was educated at Dulwich College and worked as a reporter on newspapers and magazines in England, Rhodesia and New Zealand before coming to Canada. For many years he edited a weekly newspaper in British Columbia. With his wife, Joy, he now publishes *Integrity International* newsletter and is busy with other writing also. He has published two books of poetry, *A Time for Heroes* and *The Transcendent Nation.*